Oops...

It started as a regular night for New York City restaurant hostess Ivy Sinclair, until a rowdy customer turned out to be world famous playboy Jack Everett. Thanks to the paparazzi, now the world thinks they're a couple—which couldn't be farther from the truth. But when a brooding, sexy businessman offers her a simply irresistible proposition...

Uh oh...

Just when cutthroat venture capitalist Daniel Gladwell thought he'd never close the deal with an Italian conglomerate, a simple mistake becomes the perfect opportunity. All he has to do is convince Ivy to pretend to be Jack's fiancée while on a business trip to Italy to offset Jack's bad boy reputation. As long as Daniel doesn't sabotage the plan by claiming the tempting waitress for himself...

Oh yes!

It was supposed to be a business only arrangement. But in the magic of the Tuscan countryside, neither Ivy nor Daniel can fight the attraction building between them. In the world's most romantic setting, the line between business and pleasure is one that begs to be crossed...

Books by Maggie Dallen

The Chance Series
The Accidental Engagement
The Accidental Boyfriend
The Accidental Elopement

Published by Kensington Publishing Corporation

The Accidental Engagement

A Chance Romance

Maggie Dallen

LYRICAL PRESS
Kensington Publishing Corp.
www.kensingtonbooks.com

Lyrical Press books are published by
Kensington Publishing Corp. 119 West 40th Street New York, NY 10018

First Electronic Edition: November 2015
eISBN-13: 978-1-60183-465-2
eISBN-10: 1-60183-465-9

First Print Edition: November 2015
ISBN-13: 978-1-60183-466-9
ISBN-10: 1-60183-466-7

Printed in the United States of America

Chapter 1

Ivy Sinclair thought she'd seen it all as a hostess at a hotel bar—but when a young man came running up to her with a look of panic before diving behind her hostess stand—well, now she'd really seen everything.

"Excuse me, can I help you?" she asked, looking down at the top of his head as he crouched beside her.

The young man barely looked at her. He was too busy peering around the edge of the stand toward the door. He muttered a curse as a large, brutish man wearing an intimidating scowl walked in.

"I'm not here," the young man at her feet whispered.

"Excuse me?"

"Please," he added. His eyes widened and filled with panic. Ivy couldn't help but take pity.

The large man who looked ready to kill zeroed in on her. "Where is he?"

She swallowed a lump of fear at the aggressive tone. "Where is who?" Ivy tried to keep her voice innocent but it came out as a squeak.

She cleared her throat and tried again. "I'm afraid I don't know to whom you're referring."

He leaned in closer and Ivy fought the impulse to run. "Where is Everett?" he growled.

Ivy stared down the oversized thug who was leaning over the hostess stand. She tried not to flinch even as his hot, rancid breath hit her square in the face.

"As I said before, sir, I have no idea what you're talking about."

Several guests had paused in the hotel lobby, en route to the restaurant to watch the drama unfold. The giant didn't seem to mind the attention but this job was Ivy's only source of income and she could repeat the manager's lecture on courtesy and service verbatim. But above all else, her job was to be discreet.

Ivy had to believe that meant covering for the well-dressed, albeit rumpled young man who was currently crouching behind the hostess stand, uncomfortably close to her legs. She didn't know what the hidden man had done but she couldn't blame him for hiding from the heavyset giant who loomed over her—he looked like a man who was capable of causing serious pain.

And at this particular moment he looked like he would throttle her given the slightest provocation. Ivy was a good foot shorter than the brute, with a petite frame—not exactly an even match. She tried to keep her voice soft but stern—the same tone she used to cajole Otis, her parents' German Shepherd, into his cage when it was time to visit the vet.

"I don't know what this Mr.—uh—"

"Everett. Jack Everett," the man sneered.

The name caused even more passersby to stop in their tracks. *Why did that name sound familiar?*

"I don't know what Mr. Everett has done, but I assure you I have not seen the man you described come into this restaurant."

His frown deepened into a menacing glare and she added, "If Mr. Everett comes looking for you, I'd be happy to pass along a message, Mr.—"

He leaned in even closer. "You tell Jack that if I see him with my wife again, he's a dead man."

Ivy's hands clenched at her side. That was it. She couldn't have people making death threats in her restaurant. She drew a deep breath and mustered her courage. "If you don't leave immediately, I'm afraid I'll be forced to call the police."

The burly man slammed a fist against the podium. "Listen, lady, I'll do whatever I—" His voice cut off abruptly when she snatched up the phone and started dialing, keeping eye contact all the while.

The man muttered a curse, shook his head, and backed toward the door. "You tell that little bastard I'm coming for him."

When she was certain the man was gone from view, Ivy let out a deep breath and looked down at the young man.

"You are my hero," he said with a grin.

Ivy rolled her eyes and reached out a hand to help him to his feet. "You're Jack, I presume?"

The young man paused on his knees, a lock of floppy brown hair partially covering eyes that were filled with mischief.

"If I were you, I would get out of here quick, before he comes back," she said.

He ignored her advice and grasped her hands in his. "I'm serious, I owe you my life. That guy was going to kill me."

Ivy stifled a laugh at his melodramatic tone. He looked to be around the same age as her—most likely in his late twenties—but everything from his laughing eyes to his mussed hair said he was a little boy in a grown man's body.

"In case you didn't hear, that nice gentleman would prefer that you stay away from his wife. I hope you take his advice," she added, allowing honesty to outweigh discretion for a moment.

His look was sheepish and he gave her an adorable lopsided grin but he made no attempt to deny the accusations. The man had the face of a movie star and clearly the charm and confidence to go with it. She shouldn't be surprised that he was a ladies' man. Working in a hotel restaurant she'd witnessed more than her fair share of adulterous rendezvous. She'd thought she was worldly-wise when she'd first started working at the hotel. She was no longer fresh off the bus from her tiny hometown in Ohio, but she'd still been shocked by the constant and casual affairs. Now, after two years in one of New York's swankiest hotels her scandalized disgust had given way to weary disapproval.

The young man was still on his knees and resisted her insistent tug. She was horrified to realize that the crowd of people who'd gathered to witness the earlier scene were now watching *her*—with more than a little amusement. Heat flooded her cheeks and she dipped her head. "Please stand up," she muttered.

He flashed her a wicked grin. "Not until you accept my sincere gratitude—"

"Fine, you're welcome. Now stand up, please."

"And tell me how I can repay you," he finished.

"You can repay me by standing up." Whether it was her pleading tone or the red cheeks, he did stand up—and planted a sloppy kiss on her lips.

Sputtering with surprise and embarrassment, she pushed him away and turned her face from the people who were now laughing and clapping. Ivy ducked her head, trying to hide her flaming cheeks behind a curtain of hair. She grabbed Jack by the hand and dragged him into the hallway leading to the restrooms, away from the prying eyes of strangers. "What do you think you're doing?"

"Sorry," he drawled. "I just wanted to say thank you." His eyes were wide with innocence but the unapologetic grin told her that he found her distress entertaining.

"You've said it," Ivy said with a scowl. She tugged her hand out of his and crossed her arms into her chest.

His lips twitched in what she assumed was a valiant attempt to keep from laughing. "Do you know who I am?"

Ivy blinked at the sudden turn in conversation. "According to your friend who was just here, I'd assume you're Jack Everett."

He crossed his arms and leaned back, his eyes searching her face, waiting for something—some sort of recognition, no doubt. The hotel where she worked was one of the most exclusive in the city; nearly every guest thought they were famous as well as rich. They were almost always wrong.

"Should that mean something to me?" she asked.

"Nothing," he said with a laugh. "Nothing at all. So now that we've established my name, why don't you tell me yours?"

"Ivy Sinclair."

"As in poison ivy?"

"As in The Holly and the Ivy." At his raised eyebrow, she explained. "My mom has a thing for Christmas."

"Don't tell me you have a sister named Holly," he teased. She gave a sheepish shrug and he burst out laughing.

He gave a jaunty salute as he walked back toward the hotel lobby. "Thank you for saving my life, Ivy Sinclair. I'll be in touch."

* * * *

Word had spread quickly in the hotel and less than twenty minutes after Jack left, Ivy had been summoned to the manager's office. Franklin Webster was known for being a tough boss but he kept his mouth shut through the entire tale, giving her a chance to fully explain her side of the story.

Ivy cleared her throat and forced herself to continue despite Franklin's intimidating frown. "So you see, sir, I really didn't intend to cause such a scene. I was trying my best to keep the situation under wraps. But this young man…well, I'm afraid he was a bit of a ham and he sort of made me—er, *us*—the center of attention."

When she'd finished explaining, he took his time polishing his glasses and made a show of straightening his tie. Ivy tried not to squirm in her seat. Every time she was called into Franklin's office she couldn't help but feel like she'd been called in to see the principal. More nerve-wracking since the only times she was called on to speak to the principal were when her sister Holly was in trouble.

"Ivy, do you have any idea who Jack Everett is?"

Ivy's eyes widened in surprise. "Uh, no sir."

Franklin sighed. He handed her a copy of one of the tabloids that were sold in the hotel's gift shop.

Ivy stared at the front cover, momentarily speechless. There he was— the man who'd huddled by her feet while she fended off an angry husband. He was flashing the camera that now-familiar cocky grin, one hand on the back of a supermodel as they made their way toward a waiting limo. "Tech Mogul Out on the Town," the headline read. Ivy had never taken much interest in gossip columns or celebrities and today her willful ignorance was on display.

When she looked up she saw that Franklin was watching her with a tight-lipped look of disapproval. "I'd say your Mr. Everett has a tendency to find the spotlight. Or rather, the spotlight has a tendency to find him."

Ivy let out a pent up breath. "So you're not angry?"

"No, I'm not angry. I think you handled the whole thing quite well, considering...."

"Oh, thank you, Mr. Webster," Ivy interrupted.

Franklin's lips twisted into a rare hint of a smile. "Of course. And if Mr. Everett should be true to his offer and come back to the hotel, I know you will do everything in your power to keep him...*entertained.*"

The suggestion made Ivy's skin crawl but her smile didn't falter. It remained frozen in place as her stomach churned. She had heard stories about coworkers being urged to dress more provocatively or to flirt with the guests but she never believed them to be true. She struggled to keep her voice even. "Excuse me?"

His expression remained coy. "I think you know what I mean, my dear." His gaze lowered and he studied her figure as though appraising a piece of art at auction. "My sources tell me you were quite a hit with the young man."

She forced a joking tone as she held the tabloid up before her. "From what I gather, most women are a hit with that young man."

Franklin let out a cackle that made her jump in her seat. Franklin Webster did not laugh. Everyone knew that. But at least he wasn't eyeing her like a piece of meat anymore.

He settled back into his seat. "I like you, Ivy. You're smart and you're a go-getter. This is a tough business and there aren't a lot of openings in the areas where you show an interest..." his voice trailed off and he seemed to be weighing how best to phrase the next statement. "You'll soon learn that to be considered for promotion, an employee must show that he or she is willing to go above and beyond for the company."

Bile rose in her throat. She was going to be sick. She knew exactly what he was insinuating but feigned confusion. "Mr. Webster, are you suggesting that I get involved in a romantic relationship with Mr. Everett for the sake of my job?"

Franklin's mouth opened and closed to resemble a guppy as he protested the coarse accusation. "Of course not. I would never suggest such a thing."

"Of course not," she repeated—*because that would be illegal.*

Feeling a twinge of success at having the last word, she made a move to leave the office but he stopped her.

"No one would ever make such a crass suggestion at this hotel," he said. "But I hope you keep in mind, my dear, that there are a limited number of jobs at this hotel and there is no room for employees who aren't team players."

She stopped in her tracks halfway to the door with her back to the manager. The threat could hardly be called "veiled".

Panic warred with disgust. She needed this job.

She heard the crinkle of the tabloid when he picked it up. "We're willing to overlook your antics this afternoon because we know that you are a team player. Am I making myself clear?"

Ivy resisted the urge to spin around and tell the old man where he could shove the tabloid and her job. But that couldn't happen. She could barely afford to pay this month's rent and she was drowning in debt from her stint on unemployment. And there was no way she could turn to her parents. They had enough on their plate trying to keep their house. The last thing they needed was another mouth to feed.

It was only the thought of having to run back to her parents that gave her the strength to turn around and force a smile. "Understood, Mr. Webster."

* * * *

Ivy's studio apartment in Brooklyn was tiny, but it was all hers, and for that she was eternally grateful. Particularly that evening when all she wanted was a hot bath and a glass of wine.

Hours had passed and she still couldn't get rid of the disgusted feeling. Not even a hot bath could wash it away. For what felt like the millionth time that week, Ivy considered quitting. Oh, it would feel so good. She sank further into the tub and let herself daydream about all the ways she could give her notice. In reality, she would go to bed, wake up, and do it all over again.

She'd moved to the city right after college because she'd landed a great job in an up-and-coming ad agency. But less than two years into the great new job, the recession had hit, and Ivy's entire office had been liquidated. Hers was a small branch of a large company and the closure of their office had been a necessary sacrifice for the greater good—or so she'd been told.

The hostess gig wasn't exactly her dream job but it paid the bills and it was steady work after a series of temp jobs. And it wasn't *all* bad. More and more lately she'd been called in to help the assistant manager with event planning for the hotel and she'd discovered it was something she really enjoyed. She knew there was an opening for an events manager at the hotel. If she could just keep her head down and hold her tongue with Franklin, the job could be hers.

She sighed and sipped her wine. That was a very big "if."

The front door buzzer rang just as she was stepping out of the tub. Her elderly neighbor Edith liked to stop in for a cup of tea and a chat often and she always seemed to show up at a time when Ivy craved solitude. Sleepy and wet from the bath, she threw on a robe and went to answer the door. She tried to summon a smile for her elderly friend.

"Hi Ed—" The name stuck in her throat as she faced the stranger in her doorway.

This visitor was *not* a harmless old woman.

Ivy's mouth gaped as she took in the tall man with dark hair and even darker eyes. His shoulders were broad and he wore a well-tailored suit that looked incongruous in the dingy hallway of her apartment building. Behind him stood a nondescript man with an earpiece and ramrod posture.

"Miss Sinclair?" The tall man before her smiled, causing his eyes to crinkle and eased the intimidation factor only slightly.

"Yes?" Ivy cinched her robe tighter. She was keenly aware of the fact that she wore nothing beneath her flimsy robe.

"I'm Daniel Gladwell, I work with Jack Everett. I believe you met him this afternoon?"

Ivy nodded, unable to take her eyes off of the man before her. He had the kind of chiseled features that were usually reserved for statues or actors portraying James Bond. She made a futile attempt to swipe away some of the unruly auburn curls that had escaped from the loose bun atop her head.

She closed the door a little behind her and took a step into the hallway, wary now that the surprise of finding a gorgeous man in her doorway had worn off.

"Can I help you with something?"

The man's smile grew and he tilted his chin in a charming sort of aw-shucks way, but it was all show—the look in his eyes was strictly business. "Actually, I believe you can. May I come in?"

Ivy hesitated; her small town politeness warred with practical street smarts. "I'd rather not invite strange men into my apartment."

"Of course." If he was surprised to be denied, he didn't let on. "I apologize for the late hour. Jack just informed me of this afternoon's *interaction* and I wanted to speak with you immediately."

Now Ivy was truly intrigued. "Is something the matter? Is Jack okay?"

"Oh no, he's fine. Thanks in no small part to you."

Heat flooded her cheeks under his watchful gaze. Despite his warm smile and easy demeanor, his eyes were calculating and observant. They seemed to take in everything, from her bare feet to the damp tendrils clinging to her neck.

"That's actually why I'm here, Miss Sinclair."

"Call me Ivy, please."

"I wanted to thank you in person for your assistance today. I'm sure you're aware of Jack's fame and fortune—he's easy fodder for the tabloids."

Ivy nodded, but she was sure some of the confusion she felt was evident. *Where on earth was he going with this?* She shifted from one foot to the other.

"I came here tonight because I'd like to show you how appreciative we are...."

"We?"

"My business partners and I. There is a lot invested in Jack, and his reputation."

"I see," Ivy said politely.

"We'd like to show you our appreciation for your help today and for your discretion in the future." He was watching her closely for some sort of reaction and it took several moments for Ivy to fully grasp what he was implying.

"You want to pay me to keep my mouth shut?" The words slipped out before she could stop herself.

Only a slight widening of the eyes revealed Daniel's surprise at her outburst but he recovered quickly. "Well, that's one way of putting it, I suppose."

Daniel gave her a lopsided grin, the first genuine smile she'd seen, and Ivy was very nearly charmed off of her feet.

For a moment she just stared at the man before her, unsure of how she should react. She didn't know whether she was offended or amused. Amusement won out and she startled both men in her hallway when she burst out with a great peal of laughter.

She slapped a hand over her mouth and let out a little snort as she tried to contain her giggles. "Oh, I'm so sorry, this is just too much." She waved her hand toward Daniel and the silent man behind him who was watching her with no expression. "I feel like I just stepped into a movie or something. I mean, are you seriously trying to pay me off? If I don't take it am I going to swim with the fishes?" She giggled again at her own joke.

"Ms. Sin—Ivy, I hope I haven't offended you."

"No, no, why would I be offended?" she said, still smothering a laugh. She took a step back into her apartment and started to close her door. "Thank you for the laugh, Daniel, but you don't need to pay me. I won't say a word." She held up three fingers in salute. "Scout's honor."

His forehead creased in concern as he gave her a doubtful look that said he wasn't convinced. He opened his mouth to protest, but she held up a hand to stop him.

"Look, I understand where you're coming from, I really do. But believe me when I say I have absolutely no interest in that sort of fame. And if you don't believe that, then maybe you'll understand this—the hotel has very strict rules about not speaking to the press about their guests. If I break that rule, I'd be out of a job. If you don't trust my girl scout's honor—which is sacred, by the way—then believe me when I say I would never jeopardize my job."

He studied her for a moment longer and was apparently satisfied with whatever he saw there. "I'm sorry I disturbed you, Ivy. Have a good night."

* * * *

Ivy didn't even have a chance to hang up her coat when she arrived at work the next day; she was summoned to the manager's office the moment she walked through the door.

She was stunned to find Daniel there, leaning against the manager's desk when she walked in. Both he and Franklin turned to look at her when she entered. Ivy's stomach sank. This could not be good.

Franklin was the first to react to her arrival. He threw down a copy of that morning's paper and beckoned her over to take a look. She cautiously edged toward the desk and glanced at the paper spread before her—it was open to the gossip section. Both men seemed to be waiting for a reaction so she took a step closer and looked down.

Ivy's stomach dropped and she leaned in closer, unable to believe what she was seeing. It couldn't be. There was a large color photo in the center of the page that showed Jack on his knees before her with a caption that read, "Renowned bachelor Jack Everett may finally have found his bride. Everyone wants to know—who is the lucky lady?" As if that wasn't bad enough, there was another picture just below that perfectly captured Jack's ridiculous kiss. "Brilliant billionaire smitten with his mystery woman," the caption read.

There was a little blurb beside the pictures but Ivy couldn't tear her gaze away from the image of herself looking like a woman in love. Like a woman being proposed to, no less. This couldn't be happening.... A rush of adrenaline flooded through her, leaving her shaky and lightheaded. The words blurred before her eyes. She had a feeling she didn't want to read whatever they'd printed anyways. There was no way there would be one hint of truth to any of it.

"Franklin, may I have a private word with Ivy, please?" Daniel asked.

It wasn't so much a request as an order. Ivy couldn't believe anyone would dare to kick the old manager out of his own office but Daniel seemed to be the type to take control of every room he was in. The older man, who normally put the fear of God into Ivy, looked weak and nervous beside him. Franklin nodded and hurried toward the door. Daniel's face gave nothing away but Franklin's tight-lipped grimace was more than enough to tell her that she was in trouble. When he passed her on the way out of his office he shot out a hand and gripped her arm roughly. "You will do whatever he says to make this right, do you understand me?"

Ivy nodded and swallowed. This was it—she was going to lose her job.

Daniel leaned against the desk, one leg crossed in front of the other. He was wearing another perfectly tailored suit. This one was a dark gray as opposed to the jet-black suit he'd worn the night before in her hallway but it fit just as well. He was perfectly groomed from the tidy hair to the shined designer shoes. Unlike most men she knew, he looked like he was comfortable in formal attire as though he had been born and raised wearing designer business suits.

He was watching her. His dark eyes scrutinized her every move, and despite his relaxed posture, or maybe because of it, Ivy grew unbearably tense until she had to do something.

The words came spilling out of her mouth. "I had nothing to do with that," she said, pointing to the newspaper. Her shaking hand seemed to betray her, making her look guilty rather than what she was—horrified. She instantly regretted the outburst. She hated how defensive she sounded.

Daniel nodded, his expression unreadable. "I know."

Ivy shifted uncomfortably. Well, at least he knew she wasn't the enemy here. "If you'd like for me to call the newspaper, explain what happened...."

Daniel shook his head. "Unfortunately, the situation is a little too complicated for that."

Ivy's face scrunched up in confusion. "Too complicated for the truth?"

She thought she saw a flicker of amusement in his eyes but it was fleeting. He gestured to the chair in front of him. "Please, have a seat and I'll explain."

Ivy hesitated for a moment before squaring her shoulders and perching on the edge of the chair. She tried to discreetly pull down the hem of her skirt, which suddenly felt much too short under his scrutinizing gaze.

He sat across from her and leaned over the desk with his hands folded. Every gesture, every move, was precise. This was a man who thought through everything—nothing was unintentional or improvised. Everything was planned. And the way he was looking at her now? It was clear he had a plan for her.

"As I mentioned last night, my company has a lot at stake, and it's all riding on Jack. He is the face of EverTech and his reputation has a direct impact on the business."

Ivy nodded and tried not to shift in her seat. *Just get to the point already.*

"I won't beat around the bush, Ivy."

Oh God, could he read minds?

"I am in the middle of negotiating a very sensitive merger with a company that could either make or break EverTech."

When he paused Ivy wondered if she was supposed to speak. She opened her mouth, about to ask what any of this had to do with her but he continued before she could get the words out.

"The owner of the other company, Gianni Brunelli—well, he's a bit old-fashioned. He's made it clear that he doesn't approve of Jack's current lifestyle and this latest stunt...."

He gestured to the newspaper with a pained look. When he turned back to her, she was caught in his gaze. His dark eyes were focused on her with an intensity that was frightening. She couldn't look away.

Ivy squirmed in her seat. Was he trying to torture her? She had no idea what he was getting at but the way he was looking at her, you'd think she single-handedly maneuvered the latest 'stunt,' as he put it. Ivy gripped the edge of her chair to keep calm but she was growing impatient with nerves. She'd already offered to call the newspaper, to try to explain the situation.

Maggie Dallen

"I'm not sure how I can help you," she hedged.

"The only way Brunelli will move forward with this is if I can convince him that Jack has changed. That he's a new man."

There was a brief pause and Ivy wondered if she was supposed to know what he was getting at. She found herself holding her breath as she waited for him to continue but he was either extremely fond of awkward silences or was waiting for her to respond. His eyes were studying her expression though his face was a polite mask, no emotions to be found. He was waiting for a reaction of some sort, that much was clear, but she had no idea where this was heading—only that it couldn't be good.

"Okaaay…" she stalled.

Silence broken, Daniel stood and moved to the front of the desk so he was looming over her. He crossed his arms in front of his chest and fixed his eyes on her. "You see, Brunelli doesn't want to get into bed with someone who's 'not faithful in his private life'—those are his words not mine," Daniel said.

Judging by his smirk, it was clear that this man didn't put much stock in Brunelli's beliefs or his old-fashioned values.

She blinked up at him in the silence that followed. "So, what do you want from me?"

Daniel's laugh took her by surprise. It was a deep rumble that Ivy could feel all the way to her toes. Her breath caught in her throat at the genuine smile that caused his eyes to crinkle and made him seem less intimidating but far more dangerous.

"You're a straight shooter, Ivy. I like that."

She wished his words of approval didn't affect her but she couldn't deny the warm glow that spread through her chest and left her slightly breathless.

He looked her straight in the eye. "I want you to go along with a lie, Ivy. I want you to tell the world that you and Jack are engaged and I want you to play the part of the happy fiancée until this deal is signed."

Ivy found herself staring up at Daniel and for the life of her she was unable to come up with any words. Her brain had turned to mush in her shock and she had the odd sensation that time stood still. The hum of the air-conditioner was temporarily washed out by the sound of her own heartbeat in her ears.

Daniel was eyeing her warily, his gaze fixed on her, and for a moment she thought she saw a hint of concern in his eyes. Those dark eyes that still held her captive.

He was gorgeous. Now was not the time to be thinking about this man's sex appeal, but there it was. Her heart was racing and she was no longer certain if that was due to shock or sexual attraction.

Focus, Ivy. This man wanted her to lie for him—about her entire life.

His voice startled her back to the moment. "I can see my proposition has taken you by surprise." He relaxed his intimidating stance and leaned against the desk with his hands in his pockets as though they were discussing the weather and not her life. "Don't get me wrong, we are not asking you to do anything illegal or anything that would jeopardize your values. You will be handsomely rewarded in return—my investors and I are more than willing to ensure that you are very comfortable financially in return for this favor."

"Other than lie." The words slipped out of her mouth.

Her words put a dent in Daniel's perfectly poised sales pitch. She couldn't help it. Her mother's face loomed in her mind's eye at the mere thought of lying. Her parents had thoroughly ingrained their children with the need to tell the truth, the whole truth, and nothing but the truth.

He paused and raised his brows in polite inquiry. "I'm sorry?"

She cleared her throat. "I said 'other than lie'. You said 'we're not asking you to do anything that would jeopardize your values.' And I said 'other than lie.'"

Oh Lord, she was babbling. She was repeating their conversation like a court reporter. His forehead wrinkled as if in thought for a moment but again she couldn't tell if he was amused or annoyed. Or both.

"Yes, you have a point there. I'm sure lying to your friends and family will not be pleasant but unfortunately, we can't afford to take any chances on anyone slipping up. It would be more difficult for you as well if the truth were to come out. It would not paint you in a flattering light, I'm afraid."

Panic made Ivy's heart rate accelerate. He was talking as though she'd already agreed to go along with this stunt. She shook her head. "I'm sorry, Daniel, but I'm really not a very good liar and I'm not much of an actress. I don't think I could pull it off."

"Unfortunately for us, we don't have much of a choice in who will play the lead in this particular farce." He gestured toward the newspaper. "But you will have a team of people at your beck and call to help you—I am absolutely positive you will get through this little façade with flying colors."

Ivy bristled at his know-it-all tone. Was he really trying to steamroll her into telling a life-altering lie just because it was convenient for him?

He wasn't even pretending to frame it as a question—as though it was understood that she would comply.

"Do people always do what you say?" she snapped.

The charming smile faltered. It was slight but she caught it. His perfectly poised demeanor slipped—just for an instant, but it was enough to give Ivy a sense of triumph. She had a feeling that Daniel Gladwell was rarely taken by surprise.

He recovered quickly though and his answer was brutally honest. "Yes, Miss Sinclair. They typically do." *If they know what's good for them.* He didn't say the words but he didn't have to.

Gone was the polite smile and Ivy found herself face to face with Daniel Gladwell, the ruthless business tycoon. His jaw clenched and his eyes hardened, holding her captive yet again in a disarmingly direct glare. He looked like a gladiator ready for battle. The look he gave her was so intense, she swallowed her clever retort—this was not a man to mess with.

"Honestly, Mr. Gladwell, I'd really rather go back my job—"

"Your job will not be waiting for you should you refuse my offer." He stood up straight and moved to stand behind the desk. His tone was cool and collected, at odds with the harsh words.

She tried to ignore the uncomfortable sting of unshed tears as his words sank in. She couldn't go back to being unemployed. She'd worked so hard to get where she was. She couldn't start over. And she couldn't go home. Bad investments and a housing market collapse had left her parents teetering on the edge of bankruptcy at an age when they should be planning for retirement. If she lost her job they'd feel compelled to help her but they could barely help themselves.

"That's not fair, you can't do that." Ivy's voice shook. She swallowed and tried again. "The hotel has no reason to dismiss me. I've been a great employee. Ask anyone, ask Mr. Webster."

"It's not a matter of how well you've done your job, Miss Sinclair. The hotel can't keep someone on who acts irresponsibly with the hotel guests. Not to mention, employees here are expected to be team players."

"I am responsible. And I *am* a team player." She tried to keep the tremor out of her voice. She felt like she was on the wrong end of a steamroller. She had to regain control.

She tilted her chin up and straightened her shoulders. Who did he think he was to come to her place of work and threaten her job? Maybe Franklin wasn't in her corner, but there had to be people above him.

Standing, she faced Daniel who had returned to his seat behind the desk. "You can't fire me, Mr. Gladwell. I'm sure Mr. Webster doesn't even have the final say and you have *no* say in the matter so—"

Daniel cut off her tirade before she could even gain steam. "Actually I do have quite a bit of say. My company is the majority owner of this hotel."

His words were like a punch in the gut. Her mind struggled to make sense of this new information. It couldn't be possible—could it? Maybe he was kidding. But even as she thought it, she dismissed it. The man before her clearly didn't have a sense of humor. She stared at him with wide eyes, trying to think of something to say, but she was rendered speechless. She flopped back in her seat like a deflated balloon.

With astonishing speed his cold businesslike demeanor was once again replaced by the charming smile that Ivy was beginning to know well. It was the smile of a predator before it ate its prey. "Listen, Ivy, it doesn't have to be this way. I don't want to lose you as an employee. But I also can't allow yesterday's incident to ruin a multi-billion dollar deal that I've been working on for the past two years. You can understand that, can't you?"

Ivy just stared back at him. Her mind was racing as she considered her options. She could try her luck in an unemployment office once again and pray that she'd find a new position before she lost everything. She could go back home and try to find a job there—but no, that wasn't an option. The job market in her hometown was far worse than the city and she couldn't allow her parents to help her.

"How much?" she asked. "How much would you pay me if I go along with this?"

For a moment she thought he was ignoring her. He picked up a pen and jotted something down on a piece of paper. He pushed it her way and when she picked it up, a series of zeros stared back at her. The six-figure number took her breath away. That was enough to pay her rent for the year and still have plenty left over to help her parents.

"And of course you'll get a promotion, which comes with a raise," Daniel added.

"I don't want a promotion if I haven't earned one," Ivy said, sitting up straight. She may be desperate for money, but she still had some morals.

She thought she saw a hint of a genuine smile again. Good Lord, this man's lips were hypnotic.

"On the contrary, Miss Sinclair. I've had a long talk with Franklin and it seems you have been long overdue for the promotion. I plan to have a talk with him about that." His look of disapproval actually made Ivy nervous on Franklin's behalf.

"So, do I take it we have a deal?"

Ivy swallowed down the feeling that she was taking a leap off of a high dive without checking to see if there was water below.

"We have a deal."

Chapter 2

Ivy was in a bit of a daze. She watched Daniel warily as he paced the room—he was all business as he laid out the plan. They would hold a small press conference later that day to announce their engagement and Daniel would get on the phone with Brunelli to explain the situation and salvage the deal.

Ivy's mouth opened to interrupt but Daniel kept talking, pacing the room as he plotted and planned. He eyed her appraisingly, like she was a sports car he was considering buying. "Yes, I'm sure you'll fit the role just fine once we get you the right clothing and jewelry."

Ivy raised an eyebrow at that. "Gee, thanks."

"I'll have Jack come to the hotel this morning. You two can use my suite to work out the details—come up with a story about how you first met, how it was love at first sight, that sort of thing," he said with such a dismissive air; it was clear this man did not believe in 'that sort of thing.'

Definitely not love at first sight. She smothered a laugh at the thought. But what about love at all? Despite his charming smile and gentlemanly ways, Ivy felt certain this man was most definitely not a romantic. He was all business all the time.

As if to prove her point, he switched topics to explain how her money transfer would occur once the merger was complete. "It shouldn't take more than a couple of weeks to finish this deal."

She nodded and stood up, hoping to leave that office and find a quiet spot where she could let her heartbeat return to normal. She needed to wrap her mind around the ridiculous situation she'd just gotten herself into. Daniel stopped her before she could walk out the door. "There's just one more thing, Miss Sinclair...."

When she looked back he was holding up a contract and a pen. "If you'll just sign here, our deal will be official."

Ivy's stomach churned as she took the paper and pen from his hands. She sank back into her seat to read the fine print. Once she signed there would be no backing out. No exit strategy. She would be a stranger's fiancée and this man's pawn. She swallowed thickly and tried to focus on the words before her.

She looked up in alarm at one clause. "I can't even tell my family the truth?" It was spelled out on the paper but she had to say it aloud.

She couldn't do it. She pictured her parents, her brothers, her sister Holly—she had never lied to them. Ever. They were the people she trusted most in the world and they trusted her. Could she really go weeks letting them believe she was in love and marrying a man they'd never even met? Alarm was turning to panic. Ivy forced herself to take a deep breath reminding herself, in through the nose, out through the mouth. She kept going until her eyes could once again focus on the words in front of her.

She would have to lie to the people she loved most. She tried to think about it rationally but guilt and fear made it difficult to concentrate. She couldn't go through with it. She would be hurting them. But then again, after it was all said and done, she would be able to help her family. Wasn't that worth it?

Daniel was watching her like he was ready to pounce; he would do whatever it took to get her to sign that paper. He was still playing good cop but bad cop was ready to come out at any moment.

"I'm afraid we must insist on absolute confidentiality," Daniel said. "You, me, Jack, and Franklin are the only people who know what really happened yesterday and we need to keep it that way."

"My parents wouldn't tell anyone," Ivy started to protest.

"We can't take that risk. Besides, this announcement will put you and your family in the limelight. It will be easier for them if they don't have to lie."

Ivy bit her lip but she had to agree with that last statement. Her parents were honest people. She would hate to put them in a position where they had to lie for her, even if their lies meant that their house would be saved from foreclosure. No, this was her decision. She would not drag them into this any more than she had to. She straightened her spine and took a deep breath. She had to be strong if she was going to save her parents and herself.

With that thought in mind, she picked up the pen from the desk and signed the contract with one swift, bold movement. There was no turning back now.

Things happened quickly after that. Franklin was called back into the office and, after a brief aside with Daniel, led her from the room and into a private suite on the top floor that had the most magnificent view of the city Ivy had ever seen.

"Just wait right here," Franklin said, bustling about the room out of habit, making sure everything was placed just right. "Mr. Gladwell doesn't want you to speak with anyone just yet." He turned and smiled at her, a rare and awkward gesture that revealed far more teeth than necessary.

"So am I imprisoned here or something?" The room was spacious and beautiful but it was disconcerting to know that she wasn't allowed to leave.

Franklin let out a booming laugh. "No, no, of course not. Mr. Gladwell just thinks it's best for you if you are out of sight. The press have been staking out the hotel and until you and Mr. Everett work out your, uh...."

Your lie. Franklin was too diplomatic to say it but the unspoken words reverberated in Ivy's skull.

"Our story?" she supplied.

"Yes, yes, your story. Once you've worked out your story, you're free to come and go as you please. And in the meantime, Mr. Gladwell wants you to be as comfortable as possible."

There was a moment of agonizing discomfort as Ivy watched her arrogant employer attempt to wait on her. He fussed with his tie and cleared his throat before the words came out. "Is there—uh—is there anything you'd like? Some tea or coffee perhaps?"

Ivy took pity on the man. "I'm fine, thank you Mr. Webster."

He sniffed a bit as though allergic to kind interactions. "Yes, well, you know how to get ahold of the front desk if you change your mind." He paused at the door. "Oh, and Ivy...."

"Yes?"

The old man opened and closed his mouth before finally saying, "Good luck."

She spent nearly two hours alone in the suite, pacing back and forth. She'd tried to watch TV and listen to the radio but nothing could distract her from the monumental lie she was about to tell the world. But it wasn't the world at large that she cared about—it was her family. She'd never lied to her parents or her siblings before and now she was going to tell a doozy of a lie. She wondered if they'd even believe her.

Ivy had dated several men since she'd moved to the city but no one worth mentioning—and certainly no one she cared enough about to bring home. Her family knew that she was old-fashioned. She believed in love and marriage and kids, the whole package. Would they really believe that she'd fallen head over heels overnight and agreed to marry the man without even getting to know him first? Everyone teased her for being a romantic, but she wasn't exactly impetuous or daring. That had always been Holly's role. No one would bat an eyelash if Holly got engaged on a whim, but Ivy was the stable one. Ivy was the one who had career ambitions and a life plan. No one had ever described her as impulsive. And a whirlwind engagement to a famous tech genius? Well, that definitely classified as impulsive.

* * * *

Daniel checked his watch before calling for Franklin who was hovering outside of the office door.

"Yes, sir?" Franklin said. The manager had the sort of sycophant demeanor that made Daniel's skin crawl. The numbers showed that the hotel was running smoothly but he made a mental note to dig into the manager's methods. In Daniel's experience, men like Franklin Webster couldn't command respect so they led through fear or manipulation.

Like blackmailing an honest young woman into faking a romance to seal a business deal?

Daniel shoved the thought aside. That was different. It was a one-time situation and it couldn't be helped. Besides, she would be comfortably wealthy at the end of it all. Ivy's indignant protests had grown quiet after seeing the large sum she'd earn.

Franklin hovered in front of the desk uncertainly. "Any word from Jack?" Daniel asked.

Franklin shook his head with a look of regret. "It seems Mr. Everett is running late, Mr. Gladwell."

Of course he was. Jack was always late. He might be a genius in the world of technology but apparently setting an alarm clock was too difficult for him. Daniel shoved the chair back so he could move about the room. What he really needed was to go for a run. Or swim some laps. He needed to do something physical to shake off this terrible day. But instead, he was trapped in this tiny room with Franklin hovering around him like a gnat. All so Daniel could clean up the mess that Jack had created.

Patience had never been Daniel's virtue and on a day like today, he had none to spare. Guilt gnawed at him and no amount of pacing could put him at ease. He'd just strong-armed a seemingly sweet, innocent young woman. Not his finest hour.

A corner of his mouth twitched involuntarily at the memory of Ivy sitting across from him, every emotion playing across her face for the world to see. She was open and honest—an anomaly in the world Daniel came from.

And she'd stood up to him. That never happened these days. Even the most hardened business opponents cowered before him. He'd made a name for himself by being ruthless and he couldn't remember the last time someone had the courage to challenge him to his face.

It was sexy. Nope. No. That was a road he could not go down. She was a part of the Brunelli deal now, which meant she was off-limits.

She was attractive to him because she was an anomaly, that was all. He'd never met a woman like her. She'd surprised him but he respected it. He respected her. A smile tugged at his lips when he thought of her standing up to him—she was surprisingly strong underneath that soft, lovely exterior.

But then he'd played his hand and threatened her job, squelching her arguments swiftly and without mercy. The smile died on his lips as guilt reared its ugly head once again. He'd watched pride war with desperation as she'd weighed her options. The anger and frustration she felt when she realized that she didn't have any options—she might as well have screamed out loud, it was that obvious. He'd done his homework, he'd had his investigators pull her record, do a little digging—Ivy was one paycheck away from broke. She knew it. He knew it. And he'd used that knowledge to his advantage.

Daniel heard Jack's laughter followed by the echoing chorus of female giggles coming down the hallway long before Franklin announced his arrival. When Jack made an entrance, it was with all the fanfare of a mariachi band.

Daniel shooed Franklin away with a wave as Jack plopped down into the seat that Ivy had recently vacated. He wore a pleading look that must have earned him extra dessert with dinner as a little boy. But Jack wasn't a kid anymore and it was time he took some responsibility for his actions.

"Do we really have to go through with this?" Jack asked.

"Yes." Daniel snapped his briefcase shut and made a move to stand. "Are you ready to meet your fiancée?"

"Danny," Jack started. Daniel flinched at the sound of his childhood nickname. He'd told Jack countless times he hated that name.

"Daniel," he corrected. Daniel motioned for him to get on with it.

"Let's talk about this for a minute," Jack continued, leaning forward in the chair. "This is a bit extreme, even for you, don't you think?"

The look of panic on Jack's face was almost comical. Almost. Of course he was panicking, the younger man lived for flings and excitement. The prospect of an engagement was the sort of thing that made men like Jack break out into a cold sweat.

Daniel leaned over the desk and stared down his partner. "This is not a request, Jack. This is an order. When I agreed to invest in you and your start-up, you agreed to do whatever was necessary to succeed, to make *this* business a success."

He saw Jack wince at the reminder of his failed attempts to run a business in the past. It was a low blow but it was a reminder Jack needed.

Daniel watched Jack swallow a protest. Jack knew he was right—there was a signed contract in Daniel's briefcase, ready to be brandished at a moment's notice.

"But, this girl—"

"Ivy," Daniel interrupted.

"Ivy didn't sign up for this. She seems like a sweet kid you can't drag her into…" Jack's voice trailed off as Daniel held up Ivy's contract.

"As a matter of fact, she did sign up for this. She may be a sweet kid, but she's not an idiot. She knows a good deal when she sees one."

Jack slouched down in his chair and raised an eyebrow, looking from Daniel to the contract and back again. He clearly thought Daniel was going too far. Jack seemed to be the only person in the world who didn't realize that Daniel would do whatever it took to make a deal succeed. That's why he was the best. That's why people like Jack needed people like him. They needed someone else to do their dirty work.

Daniel placed the contract back in the briefcase and stood so he was towering over Jack. "Now, if you're done complaining, are you ready to officially meet your fiancée?"

Daniel laughed at Jack's look of horror at the word fiancée. "Relax, Casanova. This is what you've been training for your entire adult life."

Jack let out a dramatic sigh but he followed Daniel to the door. "At least she's attractive."

That was the understatement of the year—the woman was hot as hell—but he let it slide.

Jack hesitated when they were just outside the suite where Ivy was holed away. "You're sure she's okay with this?"

Daniel considered his answer. "She agreed to go along with it but she's going to need your help to sell it."

Daniel opened the door and let Jack lead the way. If there was anything Jack Everett excelled at, it was making an entrance. "Hello, my darling," he called out as he strode into Ivy's suite. Daniel followed behind him and Franklin brought up the rear, though their entrance was overshadowed by Jack's brazen behavior.

Jack strode right up to Ivy, who had jumped up off the couch at the sound of the door opening, swept her into his arms, and dipped her as though they were doing the tango. When he righted her, Ivy spluttered a bit and pulled down her silky top, which had ridden up. Daniel smothered a groan. Was Jack completely incapable of making a normal introduction?

"Hello, my adorable little dummy bride," Jack said.

Open-mouthed, Ivy looked from Jack to Daniel and back again. "Your what?"

Daniel cut in before Jack could cause any more offense. "He means 'dummy' as in 'dummy corporation,'" he said. Ivy turned to him in confusion. "As in fake bride. He's saying you're—"

She threw up a hand to stop him from going any further. "Yeah, I got it."

Ivy scowled at him, apparently annoyed that he'd doubted her intelligence. She turned back to the tornado called Jack that had quite literally swept her off her feet. Even wearing the stunned expression that typically struck women when they were in the same room with Jack Everett, Ivy was gorgeous. Brunelli would take one look at her and have no problem believing that Jack had fallen head over heels.

Brunelli was a hopeless romantic, which meant he was a sucker for a good love story. The fact that he believed in love at all meant he was a sucker.

As long as Daniel kept his happy couple in check, this should be an easy sell.

* * * *

Ivy was in over her head. For what felt like the millionth time that day, she considered running away. Would anyone chase her down if she bolted? She glanced over at Franklin, who was tidying up the suite's already spotless kitchen. He seemed to be making an effort to avoid staring at the famous playboy.

Daniel was watching everything with that hawk-like stare. Including her. When their eyes met, he graced her with a hint of a smile, and Ivy felt a sudden and overwhelming case of nerves. She smoothed her shirt again to give her restless hands something to do.

"How is my beautiful bride-to-be?" Jack asked as he plopped down onto the couch and looked up at her.

Jack's eyes were warm and empathetic and he patted the couch cushion beside him. "Have a seat, let's get to know one another better." He held up his hands in mock surrender. "I promise to be a good boy."

Ivy laughed at his wide-eyed look and perched on the sofa beside him. He had it all wrong—it wasn't him she was scared of. Her eyes flicked back to Daniel, but he was fixing himself a drink at the bar and talking to Franklin, apparently giving the two lovebirds a chance to chat.

Jack lowered his voice so the others couldn't hear. "I want you to know that I truly appreciate what you're doing. I know you have your own reasons but—well, this deal means the world to me and to Danny."

Ivy noted the nickname with surprise. There was nothing "Danny" about the man she'd met. He was Mr. Gladwell and maybe Daniel to those he liked—but not Danny. Had it always been that way? Had he been 'Danny' as a kid? She was struck by an image of him as a child wearing a business suit and glowering at her and she bit back a laugh.

"People call him Danny?" she asked.

Jack's eyes were filled with a now familiar mischief. "Nobody does, except for me. Drives him nuts."

His grin was wicked and she found herself laughing along with him. Despite her best intentions, her eyes slid once more to the Danny in in question. Whatever he was talking to Franklin about, he didn't look pleased. *But he looked hot.*

Daniel glanced over and caught her looking at him. He raised his brows in a questioning look and she whipped her attention back to Jack. She hoped the heat in her cheeks wasn't visible.

Daniel was not a mind reader, she reminded herself. Why was she letting him get to her? He was clearly not her type—he was a passionless, business-comes-first, cold-hearted, ruthless—Jack's voice interrupted her rant.

"Look, Ivy, I know that my actions are the reason you're here and I apologize. Believe me when I say I never meant to cause you any harm." He gestured toward Daniel with a look of chagrin. "I never mean to cause anyone harm, but somehow I always seem to be in trouble."

He sighed loudly and looked down at his feet. Between the pout and the floppy hair that was falling into his eyes, Jack reminded her of a little boy who'd been sent to his room. It was no wonder he was such a hit with the ladies. He had boyish charm down to a tee.

She found herself laughing and he glanced up in surprise before joining in. "You're laughing because I'm such a screw-up right?" he asked, which made her laugh all the harder. He shrugged and shook his head. "I know, I know. Thank God for Danny or my new toys would never see the light of day."

She found her gaze wandering back to Daniel. Franklin was doing the talking and Daniel...was watching her. She looked away quickly, focusing on Jack but she could feel the weight of his stare.

"I take it he's the more serious of the two of you," Ivy said.

Jack rolled his eyes. "That's putting it mildly. It's always about business with 'the General'." Jack used air quotes and shifted on the couch so they were a little closer and there was no chance that Daniel could overhear.

Ivy threw back her head with a laugh. "The General, that's perfect."

As if on cue, Daniel strode in front of them, commandeering the room. "All right you two, are you ready to get down to business?"

Ivy glanced over at Jack and they both burst into laughter at the same time. Daniel's dark look only made them laugh harder.

"The General", as Ivy was starting to think of him, raised one eyebrow. "Are you finished? "Ivy and Jack shared a look and made a valiant effort to smother their giggles. Relaxing back onto the couch beside Jack, she listened to Daniel's speech about the importance of sticking to the script. She glanced over at her partner in crime and he winked at her. She knew he was only teasing but it warmed her heart. It was nice to know she had one ally on the battlefield.

* * * *

Daniel saw Jack's wink. He caught everything. That was his job. He made a mental note to have a talk with the younger man—not that it would do much good. Jack was an incorrigible flirt. But maybe that would work to their advantage in this instance. If he noticed the way Ivy's eyes lit up when Jack flirted with her, then Brunelli would too. Maybe her infatuation would help seal the deal.

Daniel was the one who'd told Jack to make it look real. If Jack could make Ivy fall for him, he should be glad. It was obvious how it would unfold. He'd seen Jack in action before. He would flirt and charm and tease and Ivy...well, she would fall for it. All women did.

Of course, knowing Jack it wouldn't last long. Jack was a decent guy but he had no attention span and he didn't do commitments. And Ivy was so clearly the kind of woman who wanted that sort of thing. She would want commitments and promises of happily ever after.

He watched her laughing with Jack as they rehearsed their stories. Ivy would fall for Jack, it was inevitable. Daniel could use any feelings she might have for Jack to his advantage—the more real her emotions, the easier it would be to sell to Brunelli. And when the deal was signed, Ivy would be left with a broken heart. He pushed that thought away. He wouldn't think about how she would feel when this was all over and she was just another notch on Jack's bedpost. He hardened himself against the pity that threatened to weaken his resolve. Ivy's future heartbreak was not his concern.

He hadn't gotten much accomplished before lunch arrived and Jack jumped up to help himself, followed quickly by Ivy, who attacked the sandwiches on the room service cart as though she hadn't eaten all day. She probably hadn't.

He pushed away a nagging feeling of guilt. The girl was in over her head—big time. There was a good chance she'd drown before this deal was through. There were so many ways she could get hurt—by Jack, by the media…by him. Ivy Sinclair would be collateral damage. That was something that came with the territory. You didn't get to his position in life without hurting some feelings along the way.

He watched her face light up with a smile at something Jack said and felt a jolt of awareness run through his body. *Damn.* This was not the time, nor the girl. Besides, she wasn't his type. In fact, she was everything he'd always steered clear of in a lover. He tended toward worldly women—the type who knew who and what they were getting involved in. They were only in it for the fun and the glamour of jet-setting around the world with a wealthy, powerful man. And he was only in it for the physical satisfaction. Once either side grew bored with the arrangement, it ended civilly. Casually even, in most cases. If one or two had held out hopes that the affair would turn into something more, he would never have known. The women he dated knew how to keep their emotions under wraps. Not like Ivy. The girl was an open book. Which was rather endearing—for someone else.

As if on cue, his traitorously perfect memory chose that moment to call up the image of Ivy in the doorway of her apartment the night before. Adorably barefoot and damp, with tendrils of her long curly hair clinging to her neck—all it would have taken was one quick move to free the rest of that hair so it would tumble down her back.

And that robe. It was simple and modest—that is, it would have been modest if it hadn't been clinging to every curve along her shapely figure.

It hadn't taken much imagination to see the delicious body that was one slip away from being exposed. It had taken every ounce of willpower he possessed to keep from pulling her into his arms right then and there.

"Okay, General, we're ready to get started." Jack's interruption couldn't have been better timed. Daniel's mind was heading into dangerous territory and he couldn't afford to be distracted from the task at hand.

He gestured for the two "lovebirds" to return to their seats on the sofa as he went over their story for a third time. He refused to leave anything up to chance.

When it was clear that his happy couple couldn't take any more 'lessons', Daniel called for a break. Jack took the opportunity to slip off to make some calls—most likely his parents to give them a heads up on the news story to come.

"Have you had chance to talk to your family and friends?" he asked Ivy.

She was sprawled out on the couch but she stiffened at the question and he knew that was her weak spot. In his line of business he always took note of people's weaknesses—even with those he was working with, who were on his side. One never knew when it would come in handy. And Ivy's reflexive response gave her away—she was vulnerable to those she loved.

"I haven't had a chance yet." She had turned her head and was staring out the window with a pensive frown. She had been alone in this suite for hours earlier in the day. She was putting off the inevitable.

"It might be easier to just get it over with."

He hadn't meant to dole out advice. It wasn't his place and it wasn't his concern. As long as she played her role, she could manage her private affairs however she saw fit. That is, as long as it didn't interfere with his plans.

"Maybe you're right," she said with a sigh. "I've just—I've never lied to my family before."

Daniel paused, struck by the simplicity of her statement. She had never lied to her family. A bitter irony washed over him. Luckily for her, she was getting advice from an expert on family betrayal.

He considered his words before he spoke, figuring out how best to play this scenario. "Lying, in this instance, would be for their own good."

She glanced up at him in surprise. "How do you figure?"

"If you told them the whole truth about your current situation, you'd be putting them in a position where they would be forced to lie. You might feel better but at their expense." He saw her brows pull together as she considered this logic.

Yes, make her feel like she was doing this for them—that was definitely the best motivation for Ivy.

He pressed on. "Not to mention, once this is over and done, you'll be able to help them financially. Don't they deserve that?"

She was looking up at him with wide eyes and for the first time he saw just how exhausted she was—physically and emotionally, no doubt. He'd done that. He was the one who had entangled her in a world of lies where she was so far out of her league.

He pushed away the guilt that threatened to devour him. "Look, we'll try to keep your name out of this for as long as possible. Your co-workers are under strict orders not to speak to the press, but it won't take long before they figure out who you are and when they do..." he let his voice trail off as Ivy gave him a nod of understanding. She couldn't hide from this forever.

They were interrupted by a knock on the door. Daniel let in a bellboy who held a small package.

"What's that?"

Daniel unwrapped the small box and brought it over to Ivy. They were alone in the room and he watched Ivy's eyes widen in understanding at the sight of the little velvet box.

It was real now, her expression said. There was no turning back.

He took her hand in his and slid the ring on her finger. She was his now, her heart and soul belonged to him—for the time being at least.

* * * *

By the time Ivy left the hotel room, she felt like she'd been brainwashed. She'd repeated her fake love story so many times, she knew it by heart, and she could almost fool herself into thinking it was real. Or maybe that was exhaustion talking.

If she'd been at all inclined to complain about Daniel's drill sergeant ways, one interaction with the press changed her mind.

She and Jack were ushered through the lobby, where members of the media had been camped out all day, waiting for a glimpse of Jack or the mysterious hotel employee who'd blasted into the limelight that morning like a bull in a china shop. No one knew who she was or where she'd come from.

When both objects of fascination stepped off the elevator, it was like Christmas come early for the press. Jack greeted them all like long-lost friends, clearly at ease in the spotlight. Ivy, on the other hand, plastered a smile on her face and prayed that it looked genuine. She saw the eyes of the reporters flicking back and forth between Jack and herself with unabashed curiosity.

"Ladies and gentlemen, I'm so glad you could be here today," he said. He wrapped an arm around Ivy's shoulder and puller her against his side while she continued to smile at the crowd like a lunatic.

"Thanks to some of your more *persistent* peers..." Jack paused as the reporters tittered. "I suppose the cat is out of the bag. The gossip pages are correct—I'm involved with this beautiful woman."

Snap, click, snap. Ivy blinked rapidly and tried not to let the smile falter in the barrage of camera flashes. She felt Daniel's eyes on her from the sidelines and that more than anything was enough to keep the smile firmly fixed.

Jack turned to look at her and for one fleeting moment Ivy nearly fell for the ruse, that's how convincing he was. His gaze screamed love and adoration. And then he winked and Ivy snapped back to reality. The boy sure could act. And he wasn't finished yet. Not even close.

"What some of you may have surmised from one photo in particular is that yesterday was a very special day for me and my lovely lady." He squeezed Ivy even tighter against his side. "I am proud and honored to announce that this beautiful woman has agreed to be my bride."

Score! Flashes popped left and right and Ivy found herself at the pointed end of a dozen microphones.

"What's your name?"

"What's the story behind the picture?"

"Did you know he was going to propose?"

"How did you meet?"

The questions came from all directions.

"How does it feel to be the soon-to-be Mrs. Everett?" one man asked.

"Where will the wedding be held?" the woman behind him asked.

The photographers seemed to inch closer and Ivy felt herself stiffen as she fought the urge to run away.

"That's all for now, people," she heard Franklin's voice boom out. He clapped his hands and made a shooing motion, effectively pushing the crowd out of the way so he could stand before them, a human barrier between the media and the happy couple.

Jack leaned over and whispered in her ear, "That's our cue. Time to leave the party, I'm afraid." He steered her toward a back exit that led into a narrow hallway where Daniel and his bodyguard were waiting.

Daniel spoke to Jack first. "There's a car waiting out back to take you to the airport."

"Right." Jack gave her arm a squeeze before taking off down the hallway. "You did well out there," Daniel said.

"Thanks. Where's he going?" She hated that she sounded so lost and lonely but that's exactly how she felt at the sight of her one and only ally running away from her.

"Don't worry, you'll see him again soon enough." Daniel's condescending tone made her grit her teeth. He gestured toward his bodyguard, the same man who'd stood silently behind him when he'd arrived at her home. "Max will take you back to your apartment."

She sighed. A little peace and quiet sounded like heaven right about now. She couldn't wait for a quiet evening of solitude to wrap her head around all that had happened today.

"You won't have much time to pack so try to stick with the necessities."

"Pack?" Ivy echoed.

Daniel and Max were already walking toward the door and Ivy hurried to keep up. "Yes," Daniel said. "You're headed to Rome tonight. The flight leaves in two hours."

Ivy's jaw dropped and she stopped walking to digest this bit of news. "Rome? Like, *Rome*-Rome? Like, *Italy*-Rome?" she called after him.

He turned to face her at the door, an amused smile formed on his lips to make him more handsome than ever.

"Just pack the necessities. We'll need to buy you a new wardrobe once we land."

"But, I can't go…" her protest died in her throat as Daniel walked out the door. She followed Max out the same exit just in time to see Daniel slide into the back seat of a town car and speed away, leaving her alone with Max. She watched his car pull away with an overwhelming sense of loneliness.

Max was already leading her toward a town car of her own and held the door for her when she approached. She smiled her thanks but it was like smiling at a brick wall, no response whatsoever.

* * * *

One hour later, Ivy was back on the road heading to the airport, a small overnight bag in her lap. She'd taken Daniel's advice and brought only the basics, some underwear and pajamas, her toiletries. Ivy brought a couple of changes of clothes but Daniel's comment about buying her a new wardrobe had stuck in her mind. She had found herself eyeing everything in her closet from his point of view. Ivy owned approximately one designer dress and it was ill-fitting and worn because she'd bought it at a thrift store. Nothing in her closet would fit the part of a woman engaged to a billionaire tech mogul. Would she be allowed to keep her new clothes when they returned from Italy?

Italy. She still couldn't believe it. She'd always wanted to go but never had the chance.

She couldn't seem to stop her leg from bouncing as they turned off onto the exit leading to airport. "Do they do this a lot?" she asked. She was about to repeat the question. Perhaps he hadn't heard.

"Do what?" Max's low voice asked from the front.

"Fly off to Europe at a moment's notice?"

She couldn't see Max's expression in the rear view mirror. "Yes."

That was the end of that conversation. She had been hoping to find an ally in Max but it was safe to say he wasn't going to be her buddy. Max steered the car off the main road leading to the airport's main terminal and headed down back roads that she never knew existed.

Ivy and her sister used to dream about backpacking through Europe—staying at hostels and eating too much pasta. Holly had gone on to travel a ton after college but Ivy never had the time or money to meet up with her. As the driver veered toward a private hangar, Ivy knew this trip would bear little resemblance to that plan. As they came to a stop beside a private jet, she let out a deep breath she hadn't realized she'd been holding.

"We're not in Kansas anymore, Toto," she muttered, making herself laugh at least. If Max heard her, he didn't let on. He grabbed her bag and she followed him to the bright lights of the jet, where the hatch was gaping open waiting for her. He set her bag down inside, ushered her in, and left without a word. She jumped when the door slammed shut behind her.

A flight attendant in a smart, navy blue uniform popped her head out of a galley and flashed her a bright smile. "Welcome aboard, Ms. Sinclair. If you'll follow me, I'll show you to your seat."

Ivy followed her through a dimly lit hallway to a small cabin that held several overstuffed leather lounge chairs.

Daniel looked up from the tablet he'd been typing on when she entered. "Oh good, you're here. Marta, tell the pilot we're ready to take off."

"But-but...."

Daniel raised an eyebrow at her panicked outburst. "Yes?"

"Where is everyone else?"

Daniel smirked and gestured to Marta to follow his orders. When she left he turned his attention back to Ivy. "Jack had to put out a fire at the office. He'll take the next flight out in the morning."

He motioned toward the chair across from him and she slid into the warm buttery leather seat just as the plane began to taxi down the runway. She gripped the armrests and tried to imagine how she was going to make it through this long flight alone in a small room with the man who had forced her into this situation. *Yup, just her and the General. Wonderful.*

Daniel smiled at her. "Come now, Ivy. Is it really so bad being stuck alone with me? I promise I don't bite."

Ivy tried to hold her tongue, she really did. But this man's arrogance and condescension were more than she could take atop her already frazzled nerves.

"It's not like I have a choice, do I?" she bit out.

Daniel watched her in intimidating silence as the plane taxied down the runway. When he spoke his voice was low and husky and it made Ivy's insides turn to hot liquid. "That's not true, Ivy. You have a choice. You always have a choice. Don't let anyone tell you otherwise." He gave a little shrug when he added, "You may not always like your options but you always have a choice."

She turned to the window to avoid facing him. She didn't want him to see her frustration. She almost hated him at that moment—because he was right and she knew it. He had put her in a terrible position, but no one had put a gun to her head. It was too late to protest and too late to change her mind. She couldn't continue to place all of the blame on this man's shoulders no matter how tempting it was. But that still didn't mean she had to like him.

Daniel had turned his attention back to the tablet in his hand. His glare would have been would be terrifying if it were directed at her. But since his anger was safely aimed at the offensive electronic device, she was free to study him without those piercing eyes watching her in return.

Okay, so he was gorgeous. There was no denying it. If Holly were here she'd be drooling right about now. But he was so not Ivy's type—he was arrogant and overbearing and there was no doubt in her mind that he could be dangerous. Extremely dangerous. She would just have to do her best to stay clear of this man until the charade was over.

Now it was her turn to glower as she looked down at the calendar on her phone. Thanksgiving wasn't too far off. What if this ruse was still going on during the holidays? How could she lie about getting married to her grandmother, for heaven's sake? She mentally reviewed the contract she'd signed. Why hadn't she thought to include an end date? Would she really be expected to play this role indefinitely?

"How long do you think it will take?"

Daniel lifted his head and she found herself fixed in his gaze like a deer in headlights. How did he do that? Was it a superpower or something?

"How long will what take?"

"This deal. Or merger, or whatever."

"I told you before, it shouldn't last more than a couple of weeks. I can't give you a specific date but I'm hopeful it will move quickly. Brunelli's moral objection to Jack's reputation is the only major holdup with the deal."

He tossed her a blanket from the adjacent seat. "Get some sleep, it's a long flight."

She pulled the blanket over her and curled her legs up so she could lean against the window. "What about you?" she asked.

His smile was self-deprecating. "I don't sleep."

Well, that answered *that* question.

Despite everything she'd been through that day, or maybe because of it, Ivy slept like a baby for the first half of the flight.

* * * *

Daniel never had a problem with his concentration. He'd always been proud of his ability to focus on work no matter where he was or the time of day or what anyone was doing around him. Until Ivy came along. Daniel caught himself watching her as she slept. He hadn't known anyone could be captivating while asleep but somehow this little imp managed it. Her innocent expression was practically angelic. Every once in a while she would shift or sigh or mutter something unintelligible. A quote from *Macbeth* came to him as he watched her. "*….the innocent sleep, sleep that knits up the ravell'd sleave of care.*"

Daniel didn't know how long he sat there entranced. Her delicate features were so perfect in the pale glow of the overhead light that it seemed a shame there were no portrait artists aboard the plane. He found himself sketching her silhouette on a napkin instead of studying the proposal his assistant had sent him. It had been years since he'd tried to draw anything other than a pie chart but the simple act was soothing and familiar. Like riding a bike.

It wasn't until the flight attendant approached him to offer a beverage that he snapped out of his idiotic pastime. Daniel crumbled the napkin and tossed it aside, annoyed beyond belief that he had allowed himself to lose track of time. Snapping open his briefcase with more force than necessary, he pulled out some documents and ordered himself to focus on the task at hand.

No woman was worth more than a business deal—no matter how fetching she looked in her sleep. With that thought firmly in mind, he focused on the contract his firm had sent for approval.

He was firmly ensconced in his work when she stretched and yawned herself awake hours later. She unfastened her seatbelt and stood up, presumably to use the restroom. She hadn't gotten far, however, when the airplane hit turbulence.

She let out a little cry before landing in Daniel's lap. He reached out to catch her but merely ended up holding her against him in a most ungentlemanly manner. Her hands were splayed across his chest and her bottom was nestled between his thighs. She gaped up at him, her breath coming in shallow gasps. His hands gripped her sides, holding her close against him as his body responded with a swift and overwhelming urgency. Her fresh, clean scent was intoxicating and her lips were there, so tantalizingly close, all he would have to do was tilt his head. He fought to control the overwhelming urge to close that gap and kiss her until she was moaning in his arms.

He knew she must have felt his erection; there was no way she could not. When she made a move to stand up and he felt her pert round breasts rub against his chest he had to clench his jaw to keep from holding her captive in his lap.

It was with considerable effort that he let her go, but once he did, she scrambled to her feet in an awkward maneuver involving two headrests and his shoulders.

"Sorry about that," she said. Her cheeks were bright red with embarrassment. "I'm such a klutz."

With that the plane gave a little jolt and he reached out his hands to steady her. He helped her into the seat beside his, smothering a laugh when she muttered a curse under her breath. "Maybe I should just stay seated for now," she said.

"That may be for the best for all of our safety." She cast him a sideways glance and he knew she was trying to tell if he was mocking her. "Did you sleep well?"

"Yes, thanks. I guess I was more tired than I thought."

"You've had a long day," he said.

He watched her out of the corner of his eye as she pulled her hair back into a ponytail and did her best to straighten her rumpled clothes. Considering everything she'd been through that day, all the shocks and major life decisions, she seemed to be coping quite well. Maybe she was stronger than he'd first thought. Maybe he had underestimated her.

"How did your family take the news?" he asked.

She looked over at him in surprise. Most likely she hadn't expected concern from him. But it was important to her, which meant it needed to be dealt with.

She looked so distraught at the mention of her family, the delicate lines around her eyes grew taut and her shoulders noticeably tensed. It was such a change from the blissfully peaceful look she'd worn in her sleep, he was almost sorry he'd brought it up.

"I couldn't get a hold of them. It's not exactly news I want to share on voicemail."

He fought the urge to wrap a protective arm around her shoulders and tell her everything would be all right.

First he was ditching work to sketch her portrait and now he was tempted to put her peace of mind before the mission at hand. He barely recognized himself. What was it about this woman that threw him so far off his game?

"You need to tell them, Ivy. The mystery woman routine won't hold up for long. We bought you a little room but it's just a matter of time before your name is revealed and the story will be out of our hands."

He was distracted by an acute stab of desire when she began to nibble on her lower lip as she considered his words. He forced himself to look away. Good God, this was not the time for an adolescent crush. He'd better find some proper female companionship once they landed in Rome—clearly he'd been without a woman for too long if this little slip of a thing could rile him so easily.

"I know you're right," she said.

"You should call them as soon as you're settled into the hotel," he said. "I'm sure they'd rather hear this news from you."

The irony of the situation—the fact that *he* was telling anyone how to deal with their family issues was comical. But this was the last hurdle. Once she lied to her family there would be no turning back for Miss Ivy Sinclair. Once she was fully on board, all he had to worry about was convincing Brunelli that their engagement was real. Daniel just had to make sure she played her part well—and if that meant never letting her out of his sight, so be it.

Chapter 3

Ivy couldn't sit still on the way to the hotel. She hopped from one seat to another in the spacious limo in an attempt to see every building and side street they passed. She caught Daniel watching her with a lopsided grin, clearly amused by her open display of awe, but she didn't care. This was her first, and possibly last, trip to Italy—she didn't want to miss a thing.

The moment the hotel came into view, Ivy knew she was entering into a whole new world. How could she ever describe this grandiose beauty to her family back home? The thought of that impending phone call was the only thing that could mar the perfection of the gorgeous palatial hotel and its picturesque setting. Daniel was right—she couldn't put this off much longer. It was time to face reality.

A bellboy grabbed her bag and Daniel escorted her through the grand lobby to the elevator banks. He seemed intent on keeping her by his side. Ivy didn't mind, especially once she discovered that he spoke fluent Italian so she could just smile and nod at the hotel employees who greeted them when they checked in.

Daniel even went so far as to take her into her room, which was down the hall from his, she discovered.

"Will you be all right here?" he asked.

Surely he was joking. Would she be all right? Who *wouldn't* be all right in this amazing sanctuary? From the plush down comforter to the romantic lighting, the hotel room was the picture of decadence. "It's beautiful," she said with a sigh.

He looked around as though seeing the room for the first time. "Yes, I suppose it is quite nice."

She laughed at the understatement and twirled around in the room that was more than double the size of her entire apartment. "Quite nice?" she echoed.

He watched her with a tolerant smile. "I suppose in my line of work, if you've seen one hotel room you've seen them all."

Ivy stopped twirling and glanced over at him. His low voice was laced with…something. Sadness? Bitterness maybe. He was always so aloof, always putting on a show for everyone around her. That comment felt like the first truly genuine statement she'd heard him utter. She perched on the bed. "You travel a lot?"

He ignored the question and began to pace around the room. "I've arranged for a shopper to come by later this afternoon with some clothing samples so we can begin to build an appropriate wardrobe."

Apparently that was the end of the 'get to know Daniel' portion of the day. Ivy sighed and walked over to set her purse down on the desk. There was a phone sitting there and its mere presence made her stomach twist in agony. She would give anything not to have to make this phone call. Ivy drew in a deep breath to steel her nerves. She had to call her parents. It would be like ripping off a Band-Aid, painful but quick. Once that was over, maybe the pit of anxiety would ease up a bit. Maybe.

Maybe later.

Ivy moved to the window, temporarily ignoring the phone. She watched the cars flying by below her window, an entire city filled with exotic foods, language and culture to explore.

"I'll leave you to get some rest," Daniel said, heading toward the door. "You must be exhausted."

She knew she should be tired but she wasn't. "I'm too excited to be tired."

He hesitated in front of the door. He was watching her; she could feel his gaze on her and felt an immediate full-body reaction at the image of his eyes raking over her curves. Curves that he knew intimately after that awful display of clumsiness on the plane.

She nearly groaned aloud in embarrassment at the memory. Not so much over her less-than-graceful show but by her ridiculous reaction to Daniel. The feel of his hard warmth pressed against her and the heady masculine smell of him, the feel of his arms around her—she'd literally been gasping for air. And he must have seen how flushed she'd become. Too embarrassing.

Daniel's voice interrupted her train of thought. "Why don't we go to the shops ourselves," he suggested. "Maybe take in a little sightseeing along the way."

Ivy nearly jumped up and down with excitement. "Yes, please. Just give me one minute to freshen up and I'll be ready." She scrambled through her bag to find a brush and lipstick.

Daniel nodded toward the door. "I'll just drop off my things and meet you in the lobby."

She stared at the phone for a moment after he left. She would definitely make the dreaded call after some sightseeing, she promised herself. Definitely.

* * * *

Maybe it was the crisp fall air or the rush of being in a foreign country, but Ivy was sure she had never known shopping could be such an exhilarating pastime. Daniel changed out of his typical suit and into a more relaxed outfit of jeans and a pullover sweater, and that alone seemed to make him more approachable. She had thrown on a casual sundress and between the new outfit and a little lipstick, she felt ready to conquer a new city.

The hotel provided a car and chauffeur for their use and Ivy was given the first-class tour. Daniel had the driver go well out of his way to ensure she got a glimpse of the city's most famous relics and museums. At each stop, Daniel regaled her with a wealth of information. Ivy was charmed. "How do you know so much about Italy's history?"

Daniel shifted a bit in his seat, the only outward sign that he wasn't altogether comfortable talking about himself. "I spent a good amount of time here when I was young."

He wasn't going to continue but Ivy pushed. "Did your family travel a lot?"

He shrugged. "A bit. My mother was born in Italy and her family was from here so we would come back often to visit."

"How wonderful! Ugh, I'm jealous. My entire family was born and raised in Ohio and we never got to go anywhere when I was young."

"Why not?"

"Money," Ivy said with a shrug. "Or lack thereof."

"I see," he said.

Ivy took in his cashmere sweater and his noble, almost entitled air. She doubted money was ever an issue in his family.

"Are you going to see your family on this trip?" she asked.

He turned to look out the window. "No." Daniel seemed to realize his answer had been a little too blunt because he turned back to her with a forced smile. "If all goes well, this deal will be over by the end of the week and we can all go home and get back to our lives."

She smiled. "Sounds good. But, since we're here…." The car had come to a stop in front of the Colosseum and she pulled him out of the car behind her so they could do a quick tour.

* * * *

Two hours, one ancient relic, and three boutiques later, Daniel pulled Ivy into a café for a well-deserved break.

"Can you believe how many cats there were?" Ivy asked. Her eyes were practically bulging out of her skull as she leaned in toward him over the tiny table.

Ivy was still talking about the damn cats at the Colosseum. He pulled her espresso cup away from her. "You are officially cut off."

"But seriously, I mean, who feeds them?"

Daniel was trying not to laugh—he really was, but Ivy's fascination with every detail of life in Rome was quite possibly the most adorable thing he'd ever seen. She was the exact opposite of the worldly, sophisticated women who ran in his circle, and it was oddly endearing.

Her enthusiasm for Italian life almost made him enjoy being back in Italy. For a little while there he had experienced the city through her eyes and not laced with childhood memories…or guilt.

"What do we do next?" she asked.

Daniel suppressed a sigh. She was endearing—and exhausting.

"We get you back to the hotel for some rest." He met her gaze over the top of his coffee cup. "You still need to call your parents."

Her eyes, which were bright with anticipation, quickly dimmed at the mention of her parents. The sheer joy on her face was instantly replaced by worry as her lips thinned into a tight line. It had been a long time since he'd met anyone who still believed in the sanctity of family and it was as admirable as it was pitiful. Daniel stopped himself from reaching out a hand to cover hers. He wanted to tell her that everything would be all right. Hell, he wanted to *make* everything all right. For a fleeting moment, he would have moved heaven and earth to bring that smile back to her face.

He almost wished he hadn't brought it up. Almost.

This was not a pleasure cruise, this was a business deal. It was altogether too easy to get distracted by the woman sitting across from him, nibbling on a biscotti. Now was not the time to let his guard down. He had a deal to make and that was the end of it. Deals came first, always. He'd set his priorities years ago, and he'd never looked back. He sure as hell wasn't about to start now.

He wanted Ivy to be happy—of course he did, a happy pawn was an easy pawn.

* * * *

Later that afternoon when they arrived back at the hotel, they were laden with bags and boxes filled with Ivy's new and incredibly expensive wardrobe as well as a few souvenirs that she'd picked up along the way.

He carried the bags to her room, setting them inside before turning to head to his own room. She followed him to the doorway and hovered awkwardly for a moment. She'd had such a pleasant afternoon, despite all the anxiety over her family, and it was all thanks to this man.

He turned to say goodbye and Ivy closed the distance between them, giving him an impromptu hug that left her senses reeling. Good Lord, the man emanated heat and practically oozed sex appeal. The first thing she noticed was how hard he was from his shoulders to his chest to his stomach. The man was built like a rock. After a second of hesitation, his arms wrapped around her in a quick, friendly squeeze and Ivy didn't want to let go.

"Thanks for a great day," she said, taking a step back. She hoped he couldn't hear how breathless she was after a mere hug.

"It was my pleasure." His smile warmed her to her core. It actually seemed genuine. Maybe he wasn't such a cold-hearted jerk after all.

She nodded toward her room. "Well, I guess I should get that rest now."

His eyes seemed darker than usual. He hesitated for a second and she thought she saw a flicker of awareness. Ivy felt her heart race as she waited, half expecting him to lean toward her or pull her close. But then it was gone and the charming but single-minded businessman was once again standing before her. His smile was impersonal. "Sleep well, Ivy."

* * * *

Ivy awoke disoriented and bleary-eyed a little while later. The bedside phone was ringing. She mumbled something unintelligible into the phone.

"Sorry to wake you."

"Daniel? What time is it?"

"It's almost dinnertime and I'm afraid your obligations are going to have to start earlier than expected."

"What do you mean?" Jet lag left her feeling like she was coming out of a coma and Daniel's serious tone made her instantly anxious. If Daniel was troubled, something was not going as planned.

"It's showtime. Brunelli called, he heard that you were in Rome. He's asked that you join us for dinner tonight."

Ivy's mouth flapped open and closed as she struggled to process this sudden change in the itinerary. She wasn't ready, she needed her ally. "But Jack—"

"Hasn't arrived yet. Yes, I know. He'll get in late tonight. I think Brunelli is looking forward to getting to know you. He doesn't want to wait."

Ivy sat up in bed and tried to shake the jet lag. "O-okay." Protesting would do no good. This is what she'd signed up for. Daniel was right. It was showtime as he'd said.

"Wear the black Armani dress we bought today. I'll be by your room to pick you up in an hour."

It didn't take her long to shower and dress, and she paced the room, watching the clock as she waited for Daniel. There was plenty of time before dinner and there was one phone call that couldn't be put off any longer. She drew in a deep breath. It was now or never.

"Hi Dad."

"Ivy! Good to hear from you. Hold on, let me get your mother on the other line." Well at least if they were both on the line she'd only have to lie once. Ivy's stomach was in her throat. She didn't know if she'd get the words out without being sick.

Her mother's bright voice joined her father's on the other end. "What's up, sweetheart?"

Like pulling off a Band-Aid, Ivy reminded herself. Once she got started, it didn't take long to get the whole story out. She tried to lie as little as possible by sticking to the facts—she'd met Jack, he was famous, they'd hit it off. He'd proposed. Boom—she was engaged. They were shocked, but after a couple seconds of stuttering and silence, they both congratulated her.

She squeezed her eyes shut, silently hating herself as she listened. Of course they were congratulating her. They'd always stood behind her no matter what choices she'd made. Her parents were incredibly supportive which only made it worse.

"Although I can't help but worry about the timing," her mother said.

"Yeah, well there were some other factors involved. But I can't really get into that now. I'll explain when I get home, okay?"

They accepted that as well as her other vague excuses with the kind of blind faith and trust that made her family so strong. Their trust in her only intensified the guilt that was threatening to eat her alive. She was going to hell.

"I just—are you sure you know what you're doing?" her father asked.

This lie was somehow the hardest to get out. *No. I am in over my head and I have no idea what I'm doing.*

"Of course." The words felt like gravel on her tongue.

She heard her mother's happy sigh. This was the day she'd been waiting for, when one of her children finally settled down and started a family of their own.

And it was all a lie.

"My little girl has met the love of her life," her mother said. "We can't wait to meet the man who won your heart."

Ivy wished someone could pull the knife out of her gut. She was the worst daughter on the planet.

The phone call had neared the end; she was telling them about her whirlwind flight to Italy, when there was a knock at the door. She let Daniel in while she wrapped up the conversation.

"Thanks for being so understanding, guys. And if the press get to be too much, let me know, okay?"

"Oh, honey, we can handle it. We're just happy that you're happy."

She smiled and swallowed down a lump in her throat. She couldn't remember the last time she'd been so overwhelmingly *un*happy. But she couldn't look to them for comfort. She had to be strong. Tears blinded her but she willed the words out of her mouth. "Yes, I'm very happy."

Ivy hung up the phone but took a moment to compose herself before facing Daniel. When she did, she nearly burst out in tears at the look of concern in his eyes. "I'm sorry, Ivy. I know that couldn't have been easy for you."

She nodded, not trusting herself to speak. Talk about understatement of the year.

"But I'm glad you decided to tell them the lie, it'll be easier for them."

She let out a sad little laugh. "That's not why I told them the lie."

He took a step closer, his brows raised in question.

There was such kindness in his gaze, such warmth, she wanted to tell him the whole truth. "I told them that because they'd be ashamed if they knew the truth," she said, her heart squeezing in pain as she spoke. "I couldn't hurt them like that."

Daniel's eyes were filled with sympathy but he didn't speak. Perhaps he knew there was nothing he could say that would ease her guilt. She was glad he didn't try. Ivy tried to physically shake off the guilt and shame the phone call had wrought by pasting on a chipper smile. She threw her arms wide and turned like a fashion model. "What do you think?"

"Gorgeous," he said, his voice was so low and his gaze so heavy she thought she might melt. "You look absolutely stunning, Ivy."

Her breath caught in her throat at the dark desire in his eyes, but the look was gone so quickly perhaps she'd only imagined it.

"Before I forget," he said, reaching into his pocket. "I've got something for you."

"Another ring?" she teased.

He handed her a cell phone. She looked up at him in confusion. "I got you one that has international service so you can call your family whenever you want."

Ivy studied the device in her hand. "Thank you, that was very thoughtful." She added, "It also makes it very easy for you to keep track of me, I presume."

Daniel's grin made her heart race. "I never took you to be a cynic, Ms. Sinclair."

Ivy laughed. "Just not as naïve as you seem to think."

He didn't try to deny it as he nodded toward the door. "Shall we?"

He held his arm out to escort her, for which she was grateful. She was not typically the type of woman who needed an escort but she was tottering on six-inch stiletto heels which, while beautiful, were by far the most impractical shoes she'd ever worn. She paused before reaching for his arm.

"Where is the restaurant? Do I need a jacket?" she asked.

He shook his head. "We're meeting Brunelli at the hotel restaurant, just off the lobby."

She stared at him in surprise for a moment before bursting out with a laugh that bordered on hysterical. "How very fitting since a hotel restaurant is where this all began." She gestured down to the designer dress and shoes, which combined cost more than her rent for two months. "Look how far I've come, literally overnight."

He held out an arm and Ivy took it, trying desperately not to lose herself in the heady feeling she got whenever he was close.

* * * *

Daniel needed to get his head in the game. He was about to put his reputation, the future of EverTech and all of their livelihoods on the line and he couldn't stop obsessing over what perfume Ivy was wearing.

After their afternoon together, which he had to admit was actually rather fun, he'd gone back to his room for a long, ice-cold shower. He would have been all right if she hadn't hugged him, pressing her soft curves against him like he was a monk or a saint or something. If she'd had any sense at all she would have kept her distance from the man who had basically blackmailed her into a fake engagement. But no—she'd hugged him.

And then he'd shown up in her room and she was all heartbroken and weepy. Worse, she was heartbroken and weepy but trying to be strong. The sight of tears in her eyes had nearly been his undoing. Her pain was like a punch in the gut and he ached to tell her that it would all work out. But he kept his mouth shut. He knew that if he started talking it would only lead to trouble. He could find himself losing the upper hand and allowing her to walk away from this farce and that was not an option.

So he'd just stood there and watched her, which was a mistake. She was so lost in her misery that she didn't seem to notice that he was all but ogling her. There was no denying that Ivy was a beautiful woman but this evening, standing there decked out in a form-fitting, sexy-as-hell dress with her auburn curls loose around her shoulders—Daniel was sure the air had been sucked out of the hotel room.

It had taken all of his will power not to pull her into his arms, crush her against him, and taste those luscious, red lips.

Instead, he forced a smile and held out an arm to escort her to the hotel restaurant on the first level. She slipped her hand through the crook of his elbow and he realized his mistake. She was too close. Her perfume was delicate and subtle and made him think of warm, summer nights in Tuscany.

All of the nerve endings in his body seemed to be rooted in the spot on his arm where her hand rested. And when she smiled up at him as they walked out the door, he nearly lost his mind and abandoned the plan altogether for one night of bliss in this hotel room.

He led her down the hallway to the elevator and forced himself to think of anything other than what lingerie she wore beneath that revealing dress. *If any.*

That line of thought was definitely not helping matters. He needed to be sharp for this dinner with Brunelli. The man was getting on in years and he often played the fool but he was still sharp as a tack. Anyone who believed otherwise was seriously underestimating the Italian tycoon.

Ivy fidgeted next to him in the elevator. She still clung to his arm, more for the balance he provided in those stiletto heels than anything else, he imagined. He'd caught her wobbling once or twice as they made their way down the hallway and had to imagine high heels were not part of her everyday wear as a hostess. She was nibbling on her lower lip as she played with the edge of her hem and straightened the straps. The poor girl was nervous and the least he could do was help put her at ease.

"Brunelli is going to love you," he said.

She glanced up at him in surprise. Uncertainty flickered in her eyes. "You think so?"

Daniel made a point of looking her up and down. "Are you kidding? Brunelli doesn't stand a chance."

Ivy smiled but gave a little roll of her eyes. She thought he was teasing her. She had no idea.

The elevator doors opened and as they stepped into the lobby her grip tightened on his arm. He looked down to see her lips pursed and her forehead creased in concern.

"What if he doesn't believe us? What if he doesn't believe that Jack fell in love with me so quickly?" she whispered.

Daniel smiled down at her. "He'll believe it. I bet you a million dollars he'll be smitten with you himself by the end of dinner."

Her eyes were still clouded with worry. Leaning down, he tried to ignore her luscious smell and the closeness of her warm skin. He whispered in her ear, "He won't stand a chance, my dear. You're utterly enchanting."

Her cheeks pinkened at the compliment and her slow smile made his chest tighten. He would definitely have to watch himself. This woman was as dangerous as she was charming.

* * * *

"Danny, my boy!" Ivy was startled by the booming voice that came from a rotund, gray-haired man who was sitting at a table near the rear of the restaurant. Ignoring the looks from his fellow patrons, the man beckoned them over.

Brunelli stood as they neared and Daniel welcomed the older man's effusive greeting with a handshake and a slap on the back. "Brunelli, it's good to see you, as always."

The older man turned his attention to Ivy and the butterflies in her stomach came to a rest. His grin was infectious and he pulled her into a bear hug before kissing both of her cheeks. "*Bella donna*, it's no wonder my boy, Jack, has lost his mind over you."

Ivy saw Daniel raise one brow in an 'I-told-you-so' look from the corner of her eye. "It's a pleasure to finally meet you, Mr. Brunelli. Jack and Daniel have told me so much about you."

"Please, please, call me Gianni. We don't stand on formality here." He pulled out a seat for her before sitting himself. "Let me introduce you to Angelo, he is my nephew and my right-hand man."

A thin, gawky-looking young man rose halfway out of his seat, gave her a slight bow and sat back down.

"You'll have to excuse Angelo, his English is not so good."

Ivy was aware of Daniel sitting beside her and was both comforted and distracted by the feel of his leg brushing up against hers when he pulled his seat in.

"So tell me, how did you and Jack meet?" Brunelli asked.

All eyes were on her, even young Angelo's, although she wasn't sure he had followed a word they said. "It all started when Jack came to eat at the restaurant where I work...."

They'd all agreed to stay as close to the truth as possible and once she got started, Ivy found herself lying effortlessly. And Brunelli ate it up. Clearly a hopeless romantic, the old man's eyes were tearing up with joy by the end.

"*Bellisimo*! Ah, that is a fantastic story, my dear." He leaned over and kissed her hand. "I am so glad you and Jack have found joy." His smile held a touch of sadness when he added, "May you find the kind of unconditional love and happiness that I shared with my dearly departed wife."

Ivy squeezed his hand in comfort and he flashed her a warm smile. She felt the ever-present guilt gnaw at the pit of her stomach. Love, real love, clearly meant the world to this big-hearted man and she was using that fact to dupe him. She was a first-class jerk. But it was too late to turn back now.

With the hard part over with, Ivy was free to enjoy the rest of the meal. And oh, what a meal. Every once in a while Daniel attempted to steer the conversation to business but Brunelli wouldn't have it. "I'm not here to discuss that, my friend. Tonight we are here to welcome the new Mrs. Jack Everett to Italy."

He and Ivy clinked glasses and she tried not to laugh aloud at Daniel's disappointment. She leaned over. "Is it really so horrible to have one night of fun?" she teased. "Lighten up, *Danny*!"

Daniel rolled his eyes at her use of Jack's nickname but after that he did seem to lighten up a bit, even sharing some amusing stories of his own about his travels abroad.

He had her laughing aloud about his first trip to China when he butchered the language so badly he accidentally insulted his host's wife. She had to admit, the uptight businessman could actually be rather funny when he wanted to be. And they way he'd listened when she was upset over her parents and given her a pep talk when she was nervous tonight? He'd actually been...*kind.*

Completely at odds with the cold man who'd forced her into this situation. Doubt niggled at her. It was hard to tell how much of his nice guy act was real. Maybe he was just trying to placate her, make her happy so she went along with his plans. She had a hard time believing that though. His concern had seemed genuine and everything he'd done since they boarded the plane had been to make her comfortable and at ease.

As the dinner progressed and Ivy's engagement was no longer the focus of conversation, she had a chance to relax and she found her mind drifting back to that moment in her hotel room before they'd headed downstairs when his eyes seemed to darken and she'd seen lust in gaze. For a brief moment he'd looked dangerous in the best possible way. She hadn't been imagining his reaction to her. Or had she?

It had been there and then gone so quickly but it had sent a jolt of sheer, mind-numbing electricity coursing through her. His desire was an aphrodisiac. Every time she thought about it, she got uncomfortably turned on. And she couldn't stop thinking about it.

Every time he spoke, she thought about it. Or laughed. Or glanced in her direction. She'd never experienced such intense sexual attraction. For the first time in her life she understood physical longing. It had nothing to do with emotions and everything to do with chemistry.

Every time he looked in her direction, she was acutely aware of her body. Sitting next to him was absolute torture. They were so close they were almost touching, but not quite. Every time his gaze turned to her, her breasts strained against her dress and she had to press her thighs together to help relieve the throbbing tension that bordered on painful. She would give anything to close that distance—to see that dark look in his eyes again. To have him give in to temptation and pull her into his arms.

She knew she should be paying attention to Brunelli and the task at hand but her body had a mind of its own as she fantasized about Daniel. She replayed that moment in the hotel room when he'd looked like he might devour her. What if instead of playing the gallant escort, he'd pulled her against him and kissed her? She imagined the feel of his lips crushed against hers. What would he do to her if he stopped being so uptight and proper all the time? She found herself doing anything she could to attract his attention.

She wanted him to notice her, to desire her, to experience the sort of visceral aching desire that made her feel wanton in a crowded restaurant.

* * * *

She was on fire.

Daniel couldn't take his eyes off of the vibrant, sexy woman beside him. She had poor Brunelli eating out of the palm of her hand. He would be next if he wasn't careful.

He glanced over at the Italian when she was telling the tall tale of love at first sight with Jack and nearly laughed out loud at Brunelli's awestruck look. The man was a romantic, pure and simple. Ivy had him wrapped around her little finger within minutes of meeting.

It was hard to imagine that a man who was so infamous in the business world could be such a sucker when it came to love and fairy tales. Daniel had discovered the notorious tycoon's Achilles heel and it was true love.

Ivy was a better liar than he would ever have imagined. If he hadn't been there to broker the fake engagement himself, he may have even fallen for her story. He would have no trouble believing that Jack had tumbled head over heels for this woman.

She was attractive, that much had been obvious since the first moment he set eyes on her. Okay, so maybe she was gorgeous. A knockout. And tonight she was the only woman in the room, as far as he was concerned. One look at Brunelli and Angelo and he knew they felt the same. It was hard to look away from her. Aside from her obvious physical beauty, she seemed lit up from within as she teased and charmed her way through dinner.

Ivy's laughter brought him back to the moment with a start. He drank a little too deeply from his wineglass and summoned the waiter to bring another bottle. Ivy turned to him with a funny little grin that made him forget how to breathe.

She dropped her voice and leaned in so only he could hear. "Admit it."

"Admit what?"

She was so close he could feel her breath on his cheek and feel her leg brush up against his. His brain was scrambled and his cock hardened instantly at the touch—Jesus, he was as bad as a teenager.

"You're having fun." She was looking up at him through her lashes, teasing him, flirting with him.

She was irresistible.

His gaze flickered to her lips, so tantalizingly close. For a split second he almost leaned in to claim her lips, the temptation was so strong.

He glanced over at Brunelli but he was talking to Angelo in Italian with dramatic hand gestures and wasn't paying any attention to them. He leaned over a little closer, so close he could smell the soft floral scent of her shampoo as he whispered back, "You caught me, I am having a good time." Before he could stop himself, he added, "Every man at this table is enthralled by your charms."

He saw her eyes widen in surprise and a flicker of awareness before she tossed back her head with a laugh that was so contagious, Brunelli and Angelo soon joined in without having heard the joke.

He drained the last of his glass. This woman was a virus that had gotten under his skin and he needed to get it out.

Dinner lingered on into desserts and then after-dinner drinks and soon the foursome were the last patrons left. Ivy and Daniel bid Brunelli and Angelo farewell and headed back to their rooms.

He should let her go ahead. He should tell her he was sticking around for one more drink at the bar. The tension and sexual frustration that had been building all night threatened to overtake him. He didn't know how much longer he could be right next to Ivy and not touch her.

Once in the elevator, Ivy leaned against the wall and her head fell back, leaving the full expanse of her neck exposed. She closed her eyes and sighed. "What a fun night."

Daniel didn't respond. He couldn't speak.

He wanted her. He wanted to taste those lips and explore every inch of her skin until she was drunk with desire. He wanted to trail kisses down her neck, to the tantalizing edge of her dress, where her breasts strained against the material. He wanted to hear her moan in delight and feel her hands on his body. He wanted to pull her into his arms and feel those curves pressed against him. He wanted to inch that sexy dress up her thighs and wrap her legs around him so he could bury himself inside of her and bring her to the brink of ecstasy.

Dear God, he wanted to take her right then and there in the elevator and he wanted it more than anything in the world.

* * * *

Ivy opened her eyes to find him watching her, his eyes darkened with desire. It was definitely not her imagination this time. He. Wanted. Her.

She couldn't seem to catch her breath as she watched his eyes caress her face and her lips before moving to her cleavage, which was exposed thanks to the dress's low neckline. Heart racing under the intense scrutiny, she parted her lips. In one fluid movement he was before her, pulling her into his arms with an urgency that would have been frightening if she hadn't felt the same way.

When his lips closed over hers she melted into a hot molten kiss that erased every thought in her mind and left only a sweet, melting sensation that coursed through her like liquid fire.

His arms tightened around her and the kiss deepened. His tongue slipped between her lips and she moaned aloud, her arms encircling his neck as she tried to get even closer to his warmth.

A ding of the elevator coming to a stop at their floor brought her back to reality with a start. She knew he felt the same when he lifted his head and quickly distanced himself from her. There was a moment of silence as they left the elevator and headed toward their hotel rooms.

All the thoughts that had been banished by Daniel's kiss were flooding her brain as she followed him down the long hallway.

What was that? It was amazing, whatever it was. Did he expect more? Would he invite her into his hotel room? And if he did, would she say yes? She wanted nothing more than to revel in the sensations she'd just experienced but the sane part of her brain was begging her to slow down.

When he stopped in front of her room, she still hadn't figured out what she wanted to happen next. Daniel decided for her. "I apologize for my behavior back there," he said, nodding toward the elevators. "I lost my head. It won't happen again."

He was so formal, so in control—so at odds with the passionate man she'd just kissed moments before.

"It's fine," she said. She offered a conciliatory smile to ease the awkward moment. She opened her mouth to say something but he had already started to head to his own room.

"Good night, Daniel," she called after him.

"Sleep well, Ivy."

Sleep well? Fat chance of that. And she was right. Despite being utterly exhausted and jet lagged, Ivy tossed and turned for hours. Her brain refused to stop replaying that kiss in vivid detail.

Chapter 4

When Ivy arrived in the hotel's restaurant for breakfast the next morning, Jack was already there scarfing down a large stack of pancakes.

"Ivy!" he called out. She went over to join him and was soon embraced in a bear hug. "I hear you were a hit last night."

He was grinning and Ivy's mood lifted in response. The knot of nerves in her belly loosened up a bit. "Where'd you hear that?"

"I saw Danny last night. He kept me up half the night hashing out details of the merger."

So Daniel had been up all night, too. She looked around pointedly. "Where is he?"

"Danny? Oh, he never eats breakfast." And just like that, the remainder of the nerves went away and Ivy began to enjoy her breakfast.

"So how'd it go when you told your family about us?" Jack asked.

Ivy recounted the conversation and Jack was sympathetic. "What about you?" she asked. "Did you talk to your family?"

He was unusually somber as he told her about his parents' reaction to the news. "My mom was so happy I thought she was going to cry," he said. "I feel terrible about how hurt she'll be when all of this is over."

Ivy winced in empathy. She hadn't even considered the fact that Jack was going through the same thing—lying to everyone he knew for the sake of money. Or at least, she assumed money was Jack's motivation as well.

"What do you get out of this merger deal?"

Jack stole a grape from her fruit cup and popped it into his mouth. "Money," he said with a grin.

So she'd been right.

"And," he added, "access to Brunelli's manufacturing company means I have a whole new playground to work on my toys." His eyes lit up with an excitement that was contagious. "I could make a working model of every idea that pops into my head. Do you know how cool that is?"

Ivy stuffed a piece of muffin in her mouth. "But you're world-famous, right? I'd bet investors would line up to work with you. And, don't take this the wrong way but…you're filthy rich, right? Why do you need to go along with this at all?"

Jack cringed. "I may be smart when it comes to technology but it turns out I'm an idiot when it comes to business. Let's just leave it at that."

She watched him eat his breakfast and was struck by his unusually serious expression. "Okay, you're right. It's none of my business. So why don't you tell me about these new toys you're working on?"

That was enough to keep Jack talking for the next twenty minutes straight.

"Sorry to interrupt." Daniel's completely unapologetic tone startled them both. He was standing over their table with his arms folded and wearing a fierce scowl.

The knot of nerves came back with a vengeance at the very sight of him. From his perfectly tailored suit to the slight cleft in his chin, the man looked like he'd stepped out of an ad for Ralph Lauren; not at all like a man who'd been up half the night working.

If there was any question of how he would act in the wake of the previous night's encounter, it was soon clear that it would not be an issue. He barely acknowledged her existence and when he did it was with his usual calm, businesslike poise.

"Jack, Brunelli expects us at his office in an hour. You'd better get up to your room and get ready. I'll meet you in the lobby in forty-five minutes." Jack scrambled to clean his plate as Daniel turned his attention to Ivy.

"You'll be all right on your own today, I assume. I've arranged for a tour guide to take you around the city but feel free to change the scheduled itinerary as you see fit."

She nodded and gave him a jaunty salute, which he ignored. He glanced down at the watch on his wrist with a frown and Ivy wondered if he was going to suggest that they synchronize their watches.

"Jack and I will meet you here for dinner tonight once we return so we can review our strategy for tomorrow night."

"Tomorrow night?" She glanced at Jack to clue her in but he was still too focused on shoveling food in his mouth to notice. Ivy turned back to Daniel, who was responding to an email on his smartphone.

"What's going on tomorrow night?"

Daniel looked up in surprise. He'd clearly already forgotten her existence at the table. "Brunelli's company is hosting a gala for charity. He's invited all of us to attend as his guests. Jack was supposed to tell you about it over breakfast." He gave Jack a withering look that went completely unnoticed.

"This will be the first time he sees you together as a couple so we have to make sure you're both prepared." He put away his phone and pointed a finger at Jack. "I'll see you in the lobby. Don't be late."

"Yes, sir," Jack mumbled through a mouth full of omelet.

Ivy watched Daniel walk away, aware of a stab of pain that she didn't want to acknowledge. She had told herself that what happened last night was wrong, that it shouldn't happen again. But if she was honest, there was a part of her—the part that had developed a crush at first sight—that had hoped last night had meant something.

* * * *

Ivy's tour that morning was fantastic—the tour guide was lovely and filled with interesting facts. She arranged for Ivy to have the best access to every museum and historic site she desired to see. But despite all that, the sightseeing paled in comparison to Daniel's tour the day before. It was like seeing the city in Technicolor one day and then seeing it in black and white the next.

When lunchtime hit, Ivy begged exhaustion and asked to postpone the rest of the sightseeing for the next day. Instead she went off on her own, strolling down alleys and side streets and absorbing the daily life in Rome. While the bustle on the streets was noisy, it was relaxing to have some time alone with her thoughts.

Ivy was not one to have flings or make out with random men in hotel elevators. Not that she had anything against that sort of thing, she just never did it. She was the good one, the stable one, and the honest one. Her family wouldn't even recognize her these days. She didn't recognize herself.

Who was that woman who threw herself into a hot, passionate kiss in a public elevator? And then lay awake all night fantasizing about the way the night could have ended?

He was right to end it when he did or at least, that's what she kept telling herself. A tipsy, one-night fling was so not what this situation needed. She was already in over her head with the lies and the acting—a secret affair would only add to her troubles.

So why was she so annoyed that he'd walked away?

It was just residual sexual frustration. And pride. It stung that he had been the one to come to his senses when she was a heartbeat away from inviting him in to her room. He'd been swept up in it, too, she knew that. But he'd managed to get back in control. Mr. Calm, Cool, and Collected, he was always in control.

And she was roaming the streets of Rome, obsessing about him like she was in junior high.

When the sun started to set she returned to the hotel but was at a loss as to what she should do. Ivy hadn't heard from Daniel or Jack all day and wasn't sure how late they would be. She was sure that they were too caught up in business to worry about checking in with her and getting an update on her sightseeing.

It was a depressing thought to realize her sole purpose on this trip was to sit around looking pretty and possibly play the role of a smitten young woman if necessary.

Ivy sighed and then let out a laugh that sounded much too loud in her solitary hotel room. Who was she to complain? Aside from the guilt and shame factor, this had to be the easiest and most entertaining way to make money she'd ever heard of. She'd been sent on all-expense-paid trip to Italy, for heaven's sake. She might as well enjoy every moment. With that in mind, she threw on her swimsuit and headed toward the hotel's rooftop pool.

The sun had already begun to set and the lounge chairs along the pool's deck had been abandoned. Ivy barely hesitated before diving in to the deep end. The water was cold and refreshing and she swam several laps to warm up. When she grew tired of the physical exertion, she switched to floating in the wide pool and watched as the stars began to appear as the sky grew dark.

Hearing a noise behind her she turned to find Daniel standing by the side of the pool, watching her. She floundered for a moment before finding the bottom of the pool with her toes. How long had he been out here?

"Sorry, I didn't mean to startle you."

Chest heaving, she stared at the man before her, mesmerized. He had no shirt on and a towel dangled from his hand. Despite the frigid water, Ivy felt heat stirring inside her at the sight of his magnificent physique. How did a man who traveled constantly stay as fit as an athlete? It just wasn't fair.

"The pool is closed for the evening, I didn't expect anyone else to be out here," he said. He gestured to a sign that was strung up near the entrance to the pool that said "Chiuso" in Italian and below it, in smaller letter, the English 'closed.' Oops.

Daniel was looking around the pool deck as though waiting for a crowd of people to pop out from behind the credenzas.

"I—uh, I was just finishing up," Ivy said. Good Lord, was that her voice? She sounded like she'd swallowed sandpaper. She cleared her throat and tried again. "What are you doing out here?"

He glanced down at the towel in his hand and his swim trunks. Ivy's gaze followed his and she forgot how to breathe at the sight of those trunks. She'd never had this kind of reaction to a man before—so visceral and illogical and…annoying. Why had her body decided that now was the time to go through a second puberty?

"I go for a swim every night before dinner." He walked a few steps toward the pool and eased himself in beside her. Somewhere in the back of her mind, which was currently cloudy with lust, she noted the fact that he didn't even flinch at the cold temperature.

They were close to one another—so very close. Ivy could smell the heady, masculine scent of his skin, even through the chlorine-filled air. There was something so intimate about being alone in a pool together. With no strangers around and only a few scraps of fabric between them. His gaze raked over her barely-clothed body. Her nipples hardened against the fabric and heat pooled between her thighs as his eyes moved slowly, openly admiring her curves. The only sound was the water gently lapping against the edge of the pool and their breathing. Her breath sounded loud to her own ears and her heart was racing with nervous excitement.

He was watching her, waiting for something. Was she supposed to speak? Her mind was agonizingly blank. Every coherent thought had been replaced by pure, unadulterated desire.

Despite the cool water, her skin was hot. There was an electricity between them that held her captive. It was drawing her in, begging her to move closer. His eyes locked with hers and she couldn't look away from the intensity of his stare. Ivy was reminded of a predator stalking its prey. The thought made her knees weak and she clung to the edge of the pool. She was going to drown gazing into those dark, stormy eyes, literally and figuratively.

The air grew tense as they watched each other in silence. Her body was throbbing with an aching need that refused to be ignored. She couldn't take it any longer. Without thinking, without even knowing she was going to do it, she gave into temptation and reached out a hand to touch that maddeningly perfect chest.

Daniel's reaction was swift and fierce. He pulled her into his arms with a deep groan and claimed her mouth with his tongue. Ivy gave herself up to the kiss and abandoned any attempt at reason. Her hands explored his muscular chest and the flat, hard abdomen beneath. She felt his muscles contract as her fingers skimmed over him and felt a surge of womanly confidence.

Before she could explore any further, he pulled her roughly against him so her hands were trapped between them as his mouth moved from her lips to her neck, causing her to moan aloud at the delicious torture.

And then his hands, which had been holding her firmly against him, began their exploration. First one hand moved up her side to cup her breast. Ivy's head fell back as she gasped for air. Through the thin, wet fabric of her swimsuit, he teased her hard nipples. His other hand moved over her back, pressing her against him so her breasts were pressed against his hard chest. She wriggled against him, trying to get closer. He growled in her ear and reached a hand around to grab her bottom. When he pulled her tight against him so he was firmly situated between her thighs, her eyes shot open. He was so hard.

And she was so ready. She moved against him and he sucked in air. His hands stilled and she found herself following suit. But it was difficult. Her hands seemed to have a mind of their own. He pulled away slightly, his head lowered as he struggled for breath. Ivy wanted to weep at the separation. At that moment, she would have done just about anything to ease the excruciating ache between her thighs.

"Someone could see us." His voice was so low she thought perhaps she'd heard him wrong.

"What? Who?" She turned to scan the empty poolside, dark in the early evening light. "No one is here."

"We can't take any chances." He pushed her away even further and pulled himself out of the pool. He reached down a hand to help her out but she pulled herself out on her own in one quick motion. She wasn't sure what had just happened but she had to fight a feeling of shame. He was rejecting her. She had been swept away by new sensations that completely shifted the world on its axis, and Daniel? Apparently, he had been worried about business. She had made a fool of herself…again.

She grabbed her towel and her few belongings and headed toward the door. "I better get inside before they turn the pool lights on."

"Ivy, wait."

Chest aching with unshed tears, she hurried through the glass door leading to the elevators, pretending as though she hadn't heard.

* * * *

Damn. That had not gone according to plan. Daniel poured himself a strong drink back in his hotel room and dried off from a cold shower. He'd needed water even colder than the pool to put out the flames from his encounter with Ivy. He refused to let himself even think about her or her perfect curves—he needed to purge her from his mind unless he wanted yet another cold shower.

He sat at the desk and tried to focus on the file his assistant had sent him. It was crucial feedback from his partners back in the U.S. yet he was unable to concentrate on the words on the screen.

He was preoccupied by Ivy's expression just before she'd walked away from him. She'd looked hurt. Rejected. He took another large swig from his glass. The fiery liquid did little to assuage his guilt but it did slow his thoughts long enough that he could allow himself to relax.

He needed this trip to end quickly. Between the sexual tension he felt every time Ivy was in the same room as him and the nagging worry that he would run into a family member or someone he knew from his past... Daniel couldn't take much more of Italy.

He shoved the chair back from the desk and paced the room while sipping his drink. It was no use trying to focus on anything but the problem at hand.

He needed to get out of this country and away from temptation. But he wasn't going anywhere until this deal was finished, which meant he needed to get the Ivy situation under control. Leaning against the window, he watched the cars pass below him, then took another sip and did what he did best. He came up with a strategy.

* * * *

The dining room was dimly lit and filled with dining couples when he strode in a little while later to meet Jack and Ivy, as planned. Daniel had banished the guilt that had threatened to consume him earlier and now was confident in his next move. He'd resolve the situation in the same manner he handled unexpected snags in the business world. Ivy was a sweet kid she wouldn't hold a grudge. He would apologize, charm her a bit, make sure her feelings weren't hurt—and then explain why a tryst between them would be a terrible idea. She was smart and practical—she'd proven that several times over—she would understand. He just had to broach the subject in the right way.

His plan would go into effect at dinner.

Jack was eating some of the bread on the table when Daniel approached. He looked around the empty table pointedly. "Where is she?"

"Ivy?"

"Of course Ivy. Who else were you expecting to meet for dinner?" The question wasn't hypothetical. Despite all of Jack's promises, experience had taught Daniel that Jack could find girls anywhere and at any time—and finding a new 'love of the moment' made him do foolish things.

Jack ignored his question and continued to dig into the breadbasket. Daniel was tempted to tell him not to ruin his appetite but caught himself in time. Jack would once again tease him about being a drill sergeant.

"She's late." Daniel took a seat next to Jack and grabbed a slice of bread before Jack could wolf it down.

"She's not coming," Jack said through a full mouth.

Daniel paused, a water glass halfway to his mouth. Surprise warred with concern. "What do you mean she's not coming? I gave her an order."

Jack tried unsuccessfully to hide his grin.

Okay, so maybe he did sound like a general sometimes but that's what it took to get things done.

"What are you going to do? Ground her? Send her to her room? Because she's already there."

Daniel toyed with his glass and tried to shove aside the nagging guilt. She was hurt. He had hurt her. "Did she say why she wasn't coming to dinner?"

Jack shrugged. "She didn't say. Maybe she's not feeling good. Maybe she's got jet lag. What's the big deal? Brunelli's not meeting up with us tonight, right?"

At Daniel's nod he continued, "Then give the poor girl a night off of girlfriend duty." He tossed Daniel the dinner menu. "Now hurry up and pick what you want already. I'm starving."

About an hour later he left Jack to finish off his dessert, making an excuse about having to be back in his room for a conference call. Truth be told, he hadn't been able to stop thinking about Ivy or their rendezvous at the pool and he knew he wouldn't be able to think about anything else until he dealt with it. And Lord knew he had plenty on his plate that needed his attention.

As he strode down the hallway toward Ivy's bedroom, he repeated his talking points—everything that was at stake, not to mention her future happiness. He was only here to clear the air, make sure Ivy was clear on her role in this charade and why nothing could happen between them. He'd have the talk and then walk away and get some actual word done. Simple.

Ivy opened the door after the first knock and all of his talking points flew out the window. She wore a lacy camisole and a pair of silky pajama shorts that did little to cover her toned thighs and rounded bottom. Her curly hair was styled into loose waves that framed her delicate features and tumbled over her shoulders. What he wouldn't give to spend one night with this woman.

He didn't know what he had expected. That she had gone back to her room to cry and eat ice cream? There were no tear-stained faces here. No sweatpants or oversized T-shirts. She looked like a supermodel. Well, a pint-sized supermodel.

And she was staring at him like he was from another planet. He had been standing there staring at her like a lovestruck teen for far too long.

He cleared his throat. "I—uh...."

What had he come here to say?

"Yes?" She was looking at him with wide, expectant eyes as she waited for him to continue.

"I just wanted to make sure you were all right."

She looked confused. "Why wouldn't I be all right?"

Yes, good point. Apparently he'd misread the situation before—here he'd been imagining that she was crying herself to sleep and instead she was...well he didn't know what she was up to in there but whatever it was, she looked fine. She looked far better than fine.

"I thought perhaps—that is, when you didn't show up to dinner, I thought perhaps you weren't feeling well."

She waved an oversized brush in front of his face. "I was blowing out my hair to get ready for the big day tomorrow. I'd rather do it tonight than in the morning. Didn't Jack tell you?" Her nose wriggled in an unbelievably adorable look of confusion. "I told him to tell you."

Daniel made a mental note to kick Jack in the behind next time he saw him. "No, I guess he forgot."

"Oh." She was watching his with an expectant look, clearly waiting for him to leave.

He told himself not to glance down. Do not do it. Do not under any circumstances let your gaze go below her chin.

Damn. She wasn't wearing a bra. He was struck speechless with lust and it took every ounce of willpower not to reach out for her. She started to inch back into her room, closing the door as she went. "Okay, well, I'm fine. So I guess I'll see you in the morning?"

He wanted to stop her. He wanted to wrap her in his arms and continue where they'd left off. No one was here in the hallway. No one would ever know.

The door shut in his face.

As he walked the few feet to his own door, he was still trying to work out what had happened.

* * * *

Ivy knew she was running late for breakfast the next morning but she didn't care. In fact, she took pleasure in knowing that it was driving him nuts. He hated to be disobeyed. Too bad, because she hated being controlled like a puppet.

Her sister's voice was tinny over the hotel phone. "So when are you going to spill? I want all of the gushy details."

Ivy's constant feeling of guilt just amplified tenfold. Holly was the closest in age among all of her siblings and they'd always shared everything. Especially when it came to their love lives.

"I can't believe you're going to marry Jack Everett. You knew I had a crush on him, right? Oh my God, if I wasn't so happy for you, I'd be totally jealous."

"Sorry, sis." This was news to Ivy, but in her defense, Holly had a number of infatuations and she changed boyfriends like most women changed shoes. It was hard to keep track.

"Are you kidding? Don't apologize. I think the whole thing sounds like a fairy tale. And you deserve the happily ever after more than anyone I know. Did you know your engagement made the front page of our paper? I thought Mom was going to faint when she saw you."

Ivy had to smile at that image. Their mother was not exactly a delicate flower.

"But enough about us, tell me about Jack. And Italy! Have I mentioned how jealous I am right now?"

Her sister was talking a mile a minute, which was the only way Holly ever spoke, come to think of it. But today the words were coming out so quickly Ivy didn't have a chance to respond, a fact for which she was eternally grateful. She just didn't have it in her to tell boldface lies about her new romance. What she really wanted to do was spill her guts about Daniel. She wanted to tell her sister every gory detail. Between the two of them, she knew they could make sense of the whole situation. But if she told her sister the truth, Holly would be forced to lie as well—not just to the press but also to their parents and siblings. It would be selfish of her to put her sister in that position.

"Listen Holly," she interrupted. "I've got to run. I was supposed to be at breakfast twenty minutes ago."

Hanging up on her sister's protests, she grabbed her purse and was heading toward the door when her cell phone rang. "Hey Jack."

"Good morning, sunshine."

"I know, I'm running late. I'll be right down."

"Actually, sweetheart, I was just calling to give you a heads up."

Ivy stopped in her tracks. "For what?"

"Daniel is on his way up to your room to get you. And Ivy...."

"Yeah?"

"The General is *not* in a good mood."

Ivy's jaw clenched. "Well, tough luck for him because neither am I."

Jack was laughing when she hung up the phone. Two seconds hadn't passed before there was a loud knocking on her door.

When she opened the door, nerves vied with anger. This was not a man to mess with. He towered over her in the doorway and fixed her with a dangerous glare before pushing his way into her room.

"After you," she muttered.

"You were supposed to be at breakfast a half hour ago."

She crossed her arms and planted her feet. "Yeah, I know. I got caught up."

He spun around to face her and she forced herself to keep a calm exterior in the face of his powerful anger. When he spoke, his voice was dangerously low. "I gave you an order. We have an agreement—"

"No," Ivy interjected, her pulse pounding. "Let's get one thing straight. I signed on to play the part of Jack's loving fiancée. That's what I've been doing and that's what I'll continue to do until your precious deal is done. But I did not sign up to be your—your *puppet*."

If he was surprised at the anger behind her words, he didn't let on. "You work for me, Ivy. That means you do what I say."

"Exactly, I work for you. You are my employer, but you don't *own* me. You can't control what I do every second of every day."

There was a brief silence as they squared off. His face was an unreadable mask. God, she hated it when he acted so cool and composed. She had seen glimpses of the real man beneath—and he was anything but cool and composed. That was the man she wanted to see.

"What is this about, Ivy?" She hesitated and he took a step toward her. "Tell me, what is this really about? It's not about my schedules or rules. Is it about last night? What happened in the pool?"

Ivy's mouth opened and closed. She wanted to bite his head off for even proposing that she was still upset about being rejected. But that would have been a lie. Yes, she hated his controlling ways but she had enough self-awareness to realize that her anger over the previous night was what fueled her fire. She was lashing out in a defensive gesture. The best defense is offense, isn't that what they say?

He took another step toward her so they were close enough to touch. If he would just reach out to her, she could be in his arms.

"I didn't mean for that to happen," he said. His voice was gentle and when she looked up into his eyes, they were surprisingly soft. Her heart ached a bit at the warmth she saw there. "But you have to know that it would never work."

"What wouldn't work?"

He reached his hands out and squeezed her shoulders in a brotherly fashion. "I think you're a sweet girl. Really, I do. And you're beautiful, there's no doubt about that."

Ivy waited for the "but" and tried to swallow down the hurt and anger. He wasn't *trying* to be rude, she told herself. But his next words hit her in the face like a bucket of water.

"But I could never jeopardize this deal over some fling. You understand that, don't you? This merger is too important to too many people."

Ivy gritted her teeth and tried to count to ten. Some fling? Some *fling*?

"I don't recall asking for *some fling*." She spit the words back in his face. His hands dropped from her shoulders as though he'd been burnt.

She took a step forward and poked him in the chest with her finger. She hated that she had to tilt her head up to look him in the face. She wished she could tower over him for once. "I wasn't the only one in that pool, you know. And I wasn't the one who initiated that kiss in the elevator, either. It takes two to tango, mister."

Her cheeks were burning and her breath was coming in short gulps. She wasn't used to temper tantrums. In fact, she was normally pretty laid back.

"You're right."

Ivy opened her mouth to argue but stopped in shock. She took a deep breath as she digested his words. She was right? Some of her burning anger seemed to lose its steam. She almost forgot her fury entirely when he cupped her face in his palms and tilted her chin so their faces were mere inches apart.

"You're right," he said again. He closed the gap between them and caught her lips in a kiss that was so gentle and so tender it brought tears to her eyes.

She had to swallow a protest when he pulled away. She didn't want to let go of that moment. He took a step back and turned to pace the room. "It was my fault. All of it." He looked at her then and she caught another glimpse of the man behind the mask. "I can't deny that I want you, Ivy. You know that I do. And it's my fault that things have gone as far as they have. But that doesn't change the situation for me. I have too much at stake. Too many people counting on me."

Ivy nodded. She might not like his priorities but she understood them. And hearing him admit that he wanted her in return was a bit of salve for her wounded pride.

He flashed her a half grin that made her knees weak. "Besides, you deserve to be with someone who will treat you right. Not an overbearing workaholic."

She swallowed an overwhelming feeling of loss and disappointment. He was right. She knew he was right—she deserved better.

"Well, thank you for being honest," she said. He seemed to be waiting for her to say more. "And I'm sorry I was late for breakfast."

* * * *

Daniel returned to the restaurant to wait and found Jack, still eating just where he'd left him. Anger washed over him at the sight of him, so charming and carefree—look where it had gotten them.

Jack spotted him and grinned. "Did you two make nice?"

Daniel dropped into a seat across from his business partner and didn't respond. He didn't trust himself to speak.

Jack's face fell. "Danny, take it easy on her. She's in a tough spot and—"

"That you got her into," Daniel finished.

Jack's eyes widened in surprise and he stopped chewing for the first time all morning. "What?"

A waitress came over and poured coffee into the empty mug in front of him, giving Daniel a moment to collect himself. When she walked away, he said, "I just think you should keep in mind that it was your actions that got her into this situation in the first place. Take responsibility for your actions for once in your life." That had come out harsher than he'd intended. Much harsher, judging by the shocked look on Jack's face.

"I didn't intend for her to get dragged into this. It wasn't me who decided that Ivy should pretend to be my fiancée. In fact, I distinctly remember saying it was a bad idea."

He was right. Daniel knew he was right. But it did little to cool the simmering anger that had been building since the moment he'd pushed her away the night before.

Jack dropped the croissant he'd been holding and leaned back to consider him. "Where is this coming from? Why the sudden anger at me?"

For the first time since they'd met, Jack seemed like the grown up at the table. He was watching Daniel with a detached amusement that was definitely not helping.

As Jack continued to study him, Daniel looked away. He was in no mood to be analyzed. He was annoyed, with Jack and with himself, but he had no desire to talk it out.

Jack had a point and he knew it. It was Daniel who'd forced her into this. If it were up to Jack, they would have come clean to the press, cleared up the misunderstanding and he would be sitting here with a different stunner on his arm and Daniel wouldn't be eaten alive by guilt.

Jack seemed to be waiting for him to speak, so he took a sip of his coffee and said what he'd been thinking, "You're right, it's my fault Ivy is involved in this. I got her into it and I intend to end it quickly, for all of our sakes. The sooner this deal is done, the better."

Jack nodded and took a sip of his coffee. "Good. Ivy is a sweetheart, she deserves better than this."

Daniel locked eyes with Jack—a suspicion was forming. "Are you interested in her?"

Jack gave him one of those lazy half smiles that all the ladies seemed to love. It made Daniel want to punch him in the face. "If you're even thinking about seducing her...."

"My fiancée, you mean?" Jack interrupted.

Rage threatened to spill out into full on violence but then Jack burst out laughing. "Come on, man, I'm kidding. Of course I'm not going to make any moves on Ivy. She's too sweet for a one night stand."

Daniel slumped back in the chair, temporarily paralyzed by the rush of adrenaline that had coursed through his body at the thought of Jack and Ivy together in bed.

Damn it. He was jealous.

Still shocked by the unusual sensation, he almost missed Jack's parting comment as he left the table. "Maybe when all this is over I'll ask her on a proper date." He slapped Daniel on the back on his way out.

He wasn't serious. Jack was never serious.

But what if he was?

He would ship Jack off to Siberia. It was that simple. Daniel would build him a lab in the middle of Siberia, send him there to build toys and make him money. Jack was no match for Ivy. He was unreliable, he didn't know how to commit…and he was funny and successful and adventurous and would one day want the kinds of things that Ivy would want. Like a family.

Maybe Jack would be the best thing that ever happened to her.

He and Jack hadn't been partners for long but long enough for him to know and respect the man. Against all odds, they'd even become *friends*.

It was decided. He would be happy for them if they started dating. Jack was a good guy, way down beneath the flaky, playboy persona. He wouldn't have chosen to invest in him if he didn't believe that. And Ivy deserved a good guy. She deserved to be with someone who loved her and could give her a future.

So why did the idea of them together make him want to hurl the table across the room?

* * * *

Jack pulled Ivy aside when she entered the lobby, where they were to meet up.

"How much trouble are you in?"

Ivy rolled her eyes. "He's our boss, Jack, not our warden."

Jack nodded. "So what you're saying is…."

Daniel was walking toward them so Ivy leaned over to whisper in Jack's ear. "No TV for a week."

Jack threw back his head and laughed loudly, drawing stares from the other guests and Daniel, who had just arrived from the restaurant.

Jack slid an arm around her shoulders and rather loudly announced their intentions to take a romantic stroll. She couldn't fault him for throwing himself into the public eye this morning—that was the whole point of today's outing—but really, the man was as subtle as a sledgehammer.

Daniel had tipped off the press that Jack Everett and his bride-to-be were going to be touring the city today. She knew Daniel and Jack were both hoping that tabloid coverage would help Brunelli buy into their little ruse and stop dawdling with the deal.

Ivy had been told that the photographers would be following them, yet she had still completely underestimated the amount of cameras that were thrust in her face throughout the day. If she had been beside anyone other than Jack, she wasn't sure she would have made it through the day. But Jack, being Jack, somehow made the whole day a hilarious adventure.

She didn't feel anything even remotely close to the sparks she felt with Daniel when he leaned over to plant a kiss on her lips for the paparazzi's sake. But he was so darn likeable and sweet that she didn't mind it either. He was harmless.

They went to the tourist attractions she hadn't had a chance to visit the day before and to some hidden gems that Daniel knew about. He was there every step of the way. Every. Single. Step. He was a shadowy figure in the background, keeping a close eye on his charges.

His constant presence made it impossible to forget their little argument that morning. She replayed the exchange countless times and never ceased to cringe when she got to one part in particular. *It takes two to tango, mister.* Had she really said that? Since when did she speak in ridiculous clichés?

She quickly found out that the best way to stop rehashing the conversation that morning and the kiss—oh, that kiss—was to throw herself into her role. Once she let go of the guilt that came with the subterfuge, she found that she was really quite a good actress.

Ivy allowed herself to flirt and giggle and share tender looks with Jack, enjoying the game of it all. She could feel Daniel's eyes on her at all times, which only made her play the part that much better. Her pride had been dealt a massive blow by the arrogant tycoon—flaunting a new, albeit fake, love interest was oddly satisfying.

When she and Jack were cozied up at a small table outside a quaint little pizzeria down a narrow cobblestone alley, she caught sight of Daniel lurking in the shadows nearby, safely out of sight of the photographers who hovered near the restaurant's entrance. Ivy felt his gaze on them and couldn't resist. She held Jack's hand and moved in even closer. He picked up on the cues and leaned over to give her a light kiss, but Ivy had other ideas. Wrapping an arm around Jack's neck, she held him to her, deepening the kiss into an intimate, lingering embrace. They only pulled apart when one of the paparazzi let out a wolf whistle.

Jack laughed at the interruption and Ivy glanced away, feigning embarrassment. When she caught Daniel's glare she knew she'd hit her target. She was playing her role for an audience of one.

Jack leaned over and whispered in her ear. "What was that all about? Don't get me wrong, I'm not complaining."

She winked at him. "If we want to sell the young lovers act, I just figured we should do it right."

* * * *

The threesome was quiet on the way back to the hotel that evening. "Do you think it worked?" Ivy asked.

"I guess we'll see in the morning." Daniel was speaking to her but his voice was so cold and his expression so severe that Jack glanced back and forth between the two of them with a look of blatant curiosity.

All three piled into the elevator and when Jack got off at his floor, the rest of the elevator ride was silent. Ivy licked dry lips as she walked the hallway to her room, every bit of her aware of Daniel's presence close behind her. Again she was struck by the image of a predator hunting its prey.

She stopped beside her door and turned to him. "Good night. I guess I'll see you at breakfast."

His expression was dark but she couldn't tell if it was anger or something else. Whatever was going on inside that head of his, he looked determined.

Taking a step inside, she went to shut the door but his hand stopped her. She glanced up in surprise.

"Invite me in." It wasn't a question. It wasn't a request. It was an order.

Ivy suddenly had difficulty swallowing. She had been playing with fire all day. Hell, she'd been playing with fire ever since she met this man. And it wasn't until that moment that she feared getting burnt.

He seemed to take her silence for an invitation and let himself into the room. He stalked over to the window and stood there looking out at the view. She closed the door and paused, not sure what she was expected to say or do.

She kicked off her shoes and padded into the center of the room. "Would you like something to drink?"

She thought perhaps he hadn't heard her because he didn't respond. When he finally spoke, it was clear he wasn't interested in beverages.

"Your performance today was impeccable."

She took a few steps closer, trying to catch a glimpse of his face from the side. "Thank you."

"One could easily believe that you really are quite smitten with Jack."

Ivy frowned now in confusion. "That was the point, wasn't it?"

He finally turned around to face her but his face was cast in shadows, making his already unreadable expression that much more enigmatic. "Yes, I suppose it was. I have to admit, you took me by surprise. I didn't realize you were such a good actress."

"Um, thank you?"

He was watching her with an intensity that was alarming. Ivy shifted from one foot to the other. She wished he knew what he was searching for when he watched her like that.

He took a few steps closer and looked straight into her eyes. Her heart rate doubled with his nearness and the intensity of his stare. "Are you that good of an actress, Ivy? Or have you developed actual feelings for our young Mr. Everett?"

Her eyes widened in surprise. So he *was* jealous. That had to be it. Giddy joy nearly threatened to envelop her and she had to squelch the desire to do a little jig right there where she stood. She feigned confusion. "I don't know what you mean."

His jaw tightened. "Clearly you're not that great of an actress. So I suppose it must be the latter."

Ivy frowned at the insult and crossed her arms in indignation. "Hey! I think I'm a pretty decent actress. Did you know I starred in my high school's production of—"

"He's not the right man for you, Ivy. I know he seems charming and witty and he's filthy rich and kindhearted...." He seemed to have lost sight of his point and Ivy raised her eyebrows in a silent question.

He wiped a hand over his eyes. The man really needed a good night's sleep and maybe even a proper vacation.

"Oh, hell," he muttered. "Maybe he *is* the right guy for you. How would I know?"

She took pity on him and couldn't suppress a grin. Never in her life had she felt more victorious. "But you don't want him to be the right man."

He looked up at her in grim resignation. "No, I don't."

She took another step closer. And then another, until she was so close she could feel his heat and hear his ragged breathing. He wanted her as badly as she wanted him. She tilted her face up and looked him in the eyes. "Why not?"

It was a demand. She needed to hear him say it.

He reached out a hand to caress her cheek and she nearly melted at the dangerous desire in his eyes. "Because I want you for myself."

She saw that he was still struggling.

"Ivy, if we do this...no one can know."

She closed the gap between them and wrapped her arms around his neck. "What's one more secret?"

Chapter 5

Daniel knew it was a mistake. He'd known from the moment he'd stepped into the room that he would have her. He prided himself on his willpower but with Ivy, he hadn't stood a chance. When she wrapped her arms around him, all bets were off. Nothing short of a natural disaster could stop him from doing what he'd been dreaming of from the moment he'd seen her damp and barefoot in her apartment doorway. It was a relief to finally give in to the desire that had been consuming him for days.

Drawing her into his arms, he lifted her up so her face was level with his own, one arm wrapped tight around her waist while the other held her delectable bottom. She met him kiss for probing kiss.

He was ravenous. Insatiable. He'd never known such all-consuming desire—the kind that clouded his mind like a drug and heightened every sense. He trailed kisses from her lips to her chin to her ear and down along the smooth, sensitive skin below her ear. When her head dropped back and she moaned his name, he knew he'd died and gone to heaven.

He needed to touch her, explore her body the way his tongue had explored her sweet lips. He laid her on the bed and took a moment to drink in the sight of his miniature goddess before coming to lie down beside her.

His hands were everywhere. Like a horny teenager, one hand fumbled for the zipper on her sundress while the other trailed over her breasts. She arched her back against him, biting her lip when his fingers found the hard nub of her nipple.

He finally managed to unzip the dress and she helped him pull it over her head as he shed his clothes. He stopped dead in his tracks when the dress hit the floor. She lay before him with her hair fanned out on the pillow and her skin milky white and satin smooth. Only a lace bra and a pair of black panties covered her. "Gorgeous," he said. His voice was so low and ragged he had to repeat himself. He leaned over her on the bed. "You are absolutely gorgeous."

She smiled up at him and he swore his heart skipped a beat. He wanted this to be good for her. He wanted to make her moan and cry out from sheer bliss. He lowered his head and began the slow exploration that started at her neck and led down past her collarbone to edge of the lacy bra.

Winding her fingers into his hair, she held him against her while his hands were busy roaming over the rounded contours of her belly and hips. She wriggled impatiently and he used one hand to push aside the material before licking and nipping at the sensitive breast. Her breath was coming in short gasps when he finally closed his mouth over her taut bud and sucked.

She gasped and arched against him and he took the opportunity to slide one hand beneath her where he could grasp her bottom and press her against him. "Oh please…please," she whispered.

He moved up to capture her mouth once more as he slipped a hand between them to stroke her and groaned aloud. So wet and so hot. He couldn't hold out a moment longer. He slipped off the remainder of her clothes and eased inside of her, into a liquid heat that felt better than anything he'd ever experienced.

They moved together in sync, a building rhythm that brought them both to an epic climax and left them panting for air.

Daniel held her afterward, dropping the occasional kiss onto the top of her head as their breath steadied and their heart rates returned to a normal pace. He felt it the moment she fell asleep. Her hands went limp against his chest and he heard her breathing deepen. He tugged a blanket over them and lay there staring at the ceiling, reveling in the feel of her in his arms. He couldn't remember the last time he'd been so content. A little while later, Daniel was fast asleep.

* * * *

Ivy woke the next morning to the sound of her phone ringing. She fumbled for it, half asleep. "Hello?"

"Good morning, sunshine." Ivy's toes curled and a slow smile spread over her face at the sound of Daniel's deep, sexy voice. "Morning."

Her sleepy brain came awake with a jolt and she rolled over in bed to the place where she'd last seen Daniel—by her side. "Wait a second, where are you?"

She could hear his low chuckle over the phone. "I had some work to do before breakfast. I didn't want to wake you."

"Oh." She fell back against the pillows, slightly disappointed that he hadn't woken her. She had a feeling waking up beside Daniel was a decidedly delicious prospect.

His voice interrupted that daydream. "You're late, you know."

"Mmmm?" Ivy snuggled under the covers, basking in the memory of their night together.

"For breakfast," he added. She glanced over at the bedside clock.

"Oh, for Pete's sake." She scrambled to get up out of bed.

"Have you ever heard of an alarm clock?"

She cradled the phone against her ear as she grabbed a pair of jeans by the bed. "I would apologize but you know very well I was a bit distracted before I went to bed last night. Setting an alarm wasn't exactly my top priority."

His laugh was better than a hot cup of coffee.

"I'll be down in one minute, don't start without me."

It was a little over ten minutes when she arrived at the breakfast table and Jack shot her a warning look. That look quickly turned to surprise when Daniel greeted her graciously, without the slightest hint of anger over her late arrival.

"How come she gets off the hook?"

Daniel ignored him and threw down the morning paper so they could both see it. There they were in the gossip section. One photographer had perfectly captured their cozy lunchtime tete-a-tete. She couldn't read the Italian caption but it didn't take a genius to figure out that their day had been a success.

"Great, so it worked," Jack said.

Daniel's reaction was not nearly as enthusiastic. "It helped." He took a sip of his coffee and Ivy found herself fascinated by the way his hands wrapped around the mug. She tried to catch his eye, hoping maybe he'd give her a little wink or share a look when Jack wasn't looking—anything to acknowledge their night together. But he was on his best behavior and Ivy was forced to wonder if last night had been a one-night thing. Maybe he'd had his fill. That thought left her feeling empty and cold for more than one reason.

Ivy placed her order with the waitress and their morning meeting was under way. Ivy only half listened for the first few minutes. It had little to do with her but was all about Jack's new technology. Every other word out of their mouths went over her head.

"As for you, Ivy. You need to go shopping." Daniel slid a credit card in her direction.

She swallowed the croissant she was chewing. "Again?"

"Tonight's gala is a special occasion. It's black tie. Nothing we bought for you will be suitable."

Ivy slipped the card into her purse. There were worse jobs a girl could have.

"You don't seem happy about it," she said.

His scowl caused Jack and Ivy to share a worried look—no one liked it when the General was in a foul mood. Daniel was absently stirring his coffee, clearly calculating. Ivy wished that for just one minute she could get a glimpse into that ever-working brain of his.

Jack tried to lighten the mood. "Come on, Danny, no one hates parties that much."

"The papers should all have been signed by now. He's stalling."

"Do you think he's having second thoughts about my project?" Jack asked. His face was taut with concern as he waited for Daniel's response.

Ivy didn't think she'd ever seen him so serious.

Daniel shook his head. "No, he still seemed enthusiastic about the project. I think it's you he's not sold on."

Ivy waved her hand at the paper, which was still spread open in the middle of the table. "But we've done our part. Everyone is buying it."

Daniel shook his head. "Everyone except for Brunelli. My guess is he wants to see the two of you together with his own eyes."

"What more does he need to see?" Jack sounded frustrated.

Ivy reached out a hand to squeeze his arm. She knew how much this meant to him. He did a good job of playing the devil-may-care playboy but there was a serious streak in him, especially when it came to his work.

Daniel was watching the two of them. "If I were Brunelli, I'd be suspicious of the timing of it all. I mean, the odds that Jack suddenly falls in love and mends his ways after Brunelli made his objections clear…."

He had a point and they all knew it. Ivy looked back and forth between her new friend and the man she was rapidly falling head over heels for and set her coffee down with a thud. "Well then, we'll just have to make him a believer."

"Yes, ma'am," Jack said with a grin. Even Daniel cracked a smile at her proclamation.

* * * *

Ivy studied her reflection in the mirror and tried to be objective. The dress was gorgeous, there was no denying that—it was a deep shade of red, with a plunging neckline. It hugged her curves before flowing down past her hips to the floor. A stylist from the hotel's salon had done amazing work with her hair and makeup and she almost didn't recognize herself. This was the first time she'd worn a gown since her high school prom and she was having a hard time telling whether she looked amazing or ridiculous.

She had been chauffeured from store to store in the most exclusive neighborhoods. It should have been an amazing day. Instead, she'd spent the better part of her afternoon either checking her phone to see if Daniel had called or texted or replaying scenes from the night before.

Ivy hadn't heard from him all day and she couldn't shake the nagging feeling that she would never see him again—well, at least not like she had the night before. Not the passionate, caring man who'd made her tremble from head to toe. She didn't want to lose that. She didn't want to lose *him*.

Ivy scowled at her reflection in the mirror. Since when had she become *that* girl? Her sister Holly had always been the boy-crazy one, not her.

There was a knock on her door. Jack was early to pick her up. She opened the door to find the most devilishly sexy man in the world standing at her door. There was no doubt about it, Daniel was born to wear a tux. Her lips parted for air as she studied him.

"Can I come in?"

Ivy stepped aside and waited for him to speak with an anxious knot in her stomach. This was it. He was going to tell her what a huge mistake they'd made and how they needed to end it before it went any further. She was already starting to formulate her argument when he surprised her by tugging her into his arms.

"You are absolutely ravishing in that dress."

Ivy exhaled in relief. Maybe he had more sense than she gave him credit for. Giving his lapel a little tug, she said, "You look awfully handsome yourself."

She tilted her head up to accept a sweet, tender kiss but pulled away before it could intensify. He tried to pull her back but she made a tsking sound. "Uh uh, my stylist will kill me if I ruin this." She waved a hand in the general direction of her hair and face.

His look of disappointment was so adorable and so gratifying it was all she could do not to throw herself into his arms. He reached out a hand to trail a finger over the edge of her bodice. Her lips parted and she had to force herself to take a step back before his wandering hands made her lose all sense of reality.

"Jack will be here any minute."

Daniel let out a little growl at that, dark desire turning to something even darker. "You're jealous," she teased.

His hand sneaked out and pulled her back against him, where she could feel the hard evidence of his desire. "Damn right, I'm jealous. I want to have you in *my* arms tonight." He leaned over so she could feel his breath against her ear. "*All* night."

Ivy giggled and wriggled against him. She'd never seen this side of Daniel. He was practically *playful*. She could definitely get used to it.

A knock on the door made them both freeze in place. "That's probably Jack," she whispered. "You know, my *fiancé*."

Daniel winced at the word and leaned down to brush his lips over hers, careful not to muss her hair or makeup. "To be continued," he whispered.

Jack burst into the room like a bull in a china shop, effectively ruining the mood. "Who's ready to par-tay?" he said, using an obnoxious frat boy accent.

Ivy laughed. "I am!"

"Oh, hey man, I thought we were going to meet you in the lobby."

"I wanted to make sure Ivy wasn't late." Daniel shot her a pointed look. "Again."

Ivy rolled her eyes and smothered a laugh at his lie.

"Ivy's in *trouble*," Jack sang. He danced up to her and pulled her into a waltz. "You, my dear, look absolutely spectacular. Has anyone told you that yet?"

"No one." Ivy laughed again as Daniel glowered at her over Jack's shoulder.

Jack was just getting started. He twirled her around and then pulled her into his arms for a melodramatic embrace. "Are you ready to be my smitten kitten, my eternally betrothed, my happily ever after, my—"

"That's enough, you two," Daniel interrupted. Ivy giggled at his gruff tone. She didn't think she'd ever tire of making him jealous.

* * * *

Ivy stepped into the ballroom and straight into a fairy tale. The vaulted ceiling was lit with chandeliers and candlelight as elegant men in tuxedos danced across the floor with glamorous women dripping with jewels.

She was Cinderella at the ball.

"Ah, my beautiful children," Brunelli called out when they entered. He gave each man a warm embrace before coming to Ivy. He held her at arms length and looked her over with an admiring gaze. "Ah, *bella donna*. You are truly the most beautiful woman in the room."

She returned his kisses. "Thank you, Gianni."

He led them further into the ballroom. "So, what do you think?"

Ivy tried to reply but found herself speechless at the extravagance that surrounded her.

Before long, Ivy and Jack were swept onto the dance floor and into the heart of the party.

If Ivy was Cinderella then Jack, of course, was the perfect Prince Charming. She saw older women look on in delight while the younger women watched with barely concealed jealousy as Jack fawned all over her—over cocktails, while eating appetizers, while mingling among the crowd and, his favorite, on the dance floor. Ivy had to admit, despite the fact that she was with the wrong date, she was enjoying herself. That is, until she caught sight of Daniel—or rather, Daniel's popularity.

Jealousy gnawed at her as she watched one glamorous woman after another throw herself at him. Maybe she was being unfair. Maybe they weren't *throwing* themselves, but they were certainly flirting. And Italian women, she soon learned, *really* knew how to flirt.

"What are you looking at, my dear?" Brunelli had found her standing alone in the crowd.

"Hmm? Oh, nothing. Just trying to find Jack. I seem to have misplaced him." This was a lie, of course. Jack had told her he was going off to find them both a glass of water. What she had been watching was Daniel dancing with another woman—an annoyingly beautiful and buxom other woman.

Brunelli was looking around as well, apparently to help her track down her errant fiancé.

"Thank you so much for inviting us, Gianni. This has truly been a once-in-a-lifetime opportunity."

He waved off her thanks. "Not for long, my dear. Once you and Jack wed…well, you know he enjoys these types of affairs."

Ivy gave him her most innocent smile. "You're right, I suppose. I guess I'll have to get used to this sort of lifestyle, won't I?" She leaned in a little closer. "But I'll always remember this night as my first gala and it will always be my favorite."

Brunelli's laugh was more like a roar and it drew curious smiles from the people around them. "I like you, Ivy, I really do. And I like Jack, too." He dipped his chin and gave her a knowing look. "And I especially like Daniel."

"What about Daniel?" Ivy started at Daniel's low voice in her ear. He was standing behind her looking positively dashing, like the hero in an action movie.

"Ah! Speak of the devil," Brunelli said.

"And he shall appear," Daniel finished. He was smiling at the older man and Ivy noted that it was one his genuine grins, not one of the polished smirks he normally wore. She also noted that she was beginning to be a bit obsessed with deciphering his different smiles. If Holly were here, she would be cracking up over her ridiculous infatuation.

Brunelli wrapped a fatherly arm around Ivy. "I was just telling this beautiful young lady how much I admire you, Daniel. Or can I too call you Danny?"

"You can call me anything you want once we're partners."

Ivy could feel Brunelli's laugh since she was still firmly fixed to his side. He wagged a finger at Daniel. "Funny boy. Funny, funny boy."

"You know he's one of my people, yes?" he asked Ivy.

At her questioning look, Daniel explained. "My mother's family was from Tuscany, which is where Brunelli lives." She didn't miss the fact that Daniel, while keeping a friendly tone and demeanor, had gone strangely stiff beside her at the mention of his family.

Brunelli was beaming at her. "Ah, it is the most beautiful place in all the land. You have been, no?"

Ivy shook her head. "No, this is my first trip to Italy."

Brunelli fixed Daniel with a mock glare. "This is a tragedy, my friend. You must take this charming young woman to Tuscany." Before Daniel or Ivy could respond, he barreled on. "All three of you will come to stay at my home. I insist." Daniel began to protest but Brunelli held up a hand to cut him off. When he spoke his voice was firm and there was no mistaking his meaning. "I insist. You will all come to my home. Only there will I make my final decision regarding the merger."

She saw Daniel's jaw clench but he was perfectly poised when he bowed his head in a gracious gesture. "We would be honored to be your guests."

When Brunelli turned to her she pasted on a smile. Much as she loved Italy, she had been hoping that this hoax would be over soon for so many reasons. She couldn't even let herself think about her parents—the longer this went on the harder it would be to tell them the truth and the more hurt they would be.

Who was she kidding? She was living a lie—they would be hurt no matter what. Even so, for her own peace of mind she needed this deception to come to an end.

And then there was Daniel—arrogant, commanding, charming, intelligent, funny, passionate, and insanely sexy Daniel. She wanted him more than she'd ever wanted anything in her life. And not just physically.

She wanted to go on a date with him. A proper date. She wanted to flirt with him whenever and wherever she wanted. She wanted to get to know him so well that she never had to see that stupid phony smirk ever again. She wanted to introduce him to her friends and watch him charm the socks off of her family. She wanted a relationship, plain and simple. But how could they be together if they were forced to keep their affair a secret?

Jack joined them and broke what was about to become a tense silence. He slapped a hand on Brunelli's back, wrapped a possessive arm around her waist and began a conversation about the political official who'd stopped to talk to him in the lavatory—while he was going to the bathroom.

Soon they were all laughing and the awkward moment had passed.

* * * *

The foursome drank wine and chatted for a little while until Brunelli asked to have a word alone with Jack to discuss some details of the project he was working on. "Daniel, please, escort this *bella donna* onto the dance floor. Ivy looks so beautiful when she's dancing."

Ivy laughed at the over-the-top flattery but neither could refuse when he added, "Please, indulge an old man."

So Daniel gave Ivy a gallant bow and proffered his arm, which she accepted with a little curtsy. Never forgetting their roles, Ivy cast Jack a loving look before gliding onto the dance floor and Daniel joked, "I'll take good care of her."

Once on the dance floor, Ivy melted into his arms with a sigh. This was where she belonged. This was the man who made her heart race but he was also the man who infuriated her and challenged her and held her while she slept. This was the man she was falling in love with.

She nearly lost her footing as the word took root in her mind. *Could it be?* His arms tightened around her as he moved in time with the music. There was no doubt in her mind—this was her home. Here in his arms, this was where she always wanted to be. She was falling in love.

She allowed herself a moment to indulge in the new realization and when she looked up, she found him studying her with an unusually solemn expression.

"Is everything all right?"

He smiled down at her and leaned in a bit so no one around them could hear. "Perfect now that I finally get to dance with you."

"What, Miss Botox in the green strapless number didn't have good rhythm?"

His arms around her tightened a bit and she could feel the rumble of his laugh as their upper bodies momentarily pressed together. "So I'm not the only one who gets jealous. Good to know."

"Don't let it go to your head."

They both pretended to be serious for a moment before bursting into laughter. The music changed and he led them effortlessly into a new step, one that allowed him to hold her a bit closer as they swayed in time to the music.

His voice was low and soft. "You know you are the most enchanting woman in this room, don't you?" She opened her mouth to speak but he unexpectedly twirled her and brought her back, making her laugh even more.

He watched her laugh with a warmth in his eyes that made her heart pound and the rest of the room disappear. He smiled then, a genuine, tender, almost sad sort of smile. "You may just be the most enchanting woman I've ever met."

They were interrupted by Jack who tapped Daniel on the shoulder. "May I cut in?" They were both brought to their senses and Daniel was quick to let her go. They had come dangerously close to outing themselves; they had been so lost in one another that they'd almost forgotten where they were and why. And if *she* knew it than Daniel—

"It's time for me to say good night."

She hid her disappointment when she kissed his cheek. "Good night, Daniel. See you in the morning."

But she didn't have to wait until morning. A limo dropped her and Jack off at the hotel and they said good night in the elevator. She almost let out a shriek when she opened her door and caught a glimpse of movement near the window.

Daniel was sitting in an armchair, cast in the shadows of a dim desk lamp. "How did you get in here?"

He held up a key card. "I paid for the room, remember? I suppose the front desk thinks that warrants a key of my own."

Planting her hands on her hips, she pretended to be angry. "I'll have to have a talk with the front desk. *And* security."

He ignored her teasing. "Just stand there for one moment. I want to take a look at you. I was trying all night not to stare. Do you know how difficult that was when you were there, looking like that?"

His words made her heart flutter in her chest with pleasure. She struck a model's pose. "What, this old thing?"

Even in the shadows she could see the desire in his eyes and her own body grew warm in response. Every part of her was sensitive, primed for his touch. Moving her hands along her sides, down to her waist, she saw his eyes narrow as he followed her every move. She licked her lips, excited but slightly nervous. Turning to the side she slowly—oh so slowly—inched the zipper down.

Ivy heard a hiss as he sucked in air and her confidence grew. She let the soft material slide down, slowly revealing the strapless black bra. When she let it fall to the floor with a whoosh, she heard his groan and smiled. She had bought the garter belt and barely-there panties for this moment and it had been worth every penny.

"Turn around."

She did as he asked, slowly turning so he could get his fill. Her hands reached out to pluck one of the many hairpins that held her locks in place.

"Let me do that." He patted his knee and she willingly obliged, perching herself on his knee, tantalizingly close to his warmth. She had no idea that letting her hair down could be such a sensual act.

He took his time, placing gentle little kisses along her neck and shoulders as he went along. His free hand trailed along her hip and inner thigh until she was on the brink of screaming from the sweet torture.

When every last hairpin was out and her curls tumbled down her back, only then did he turn her toward him and kiss her with all the pent-up passion they'd been suppressing all night. His hands quickly did away with the strapless number and soon he was cradling her breasts in his palm as she arched against him, silently begging for more. He was quick to oblige and with a few swift motions he had her undressed and straddling him on the chair. When she took him inside of her, she knew that at that moment at least, he was all hers.

* * * *

The next morning, Daniel was propped up in Ivy's bed, watching her brush her hair in front of the mirror. How did anyone look so beautiful in the morning? Somehow Ivy made puffy eyes and bedhead look sexy.

"I suppose I should pack my belongings. How long do you think we'll be in Tuscany?" she asked.

At the mention of his home, Daniel's entire body stiffened. Something was not right. There was no need for a trip up north and everything about Brunelli's nonchalant offer of hosting them screamed "trap".

Maybe he was being paranoid. Maybe it was just the dread of running into the family he abandoned that had him on edge. This was not good.

The threat of seeing family, not to mention his incredibly ill-advised affair with Ivy...he was so far off his game he couldn't even see the ballpark.

He came back to the present when he spotted Ivy watching him in the mirror with a look of concern. His heart did a funny squeeze. When was the last time someone had worried about him?

"What is it, Daniel?"

His attention snapped back to Brunelli and the long days that lay ahead. "I can't believe he's doing this."

"Doing what?"

"Stalling," Daniel said. "He should have signed on the dotted line days ago. I don't know what he's waiting for."

"Jack said he wants to show him the facilities, introduce him to his team. Maybe that's all it is—maybe he just wants to make sure it'll be a good fit."

Daniel nearly groaned aloud at her naiveté and with Jack's. Neither of them understood the world he lived in. "I need this deal to happen, Ivy. I've got everything riding on it."

She looked surprised by his urgency and her sweet innocence just reinforced the fact that he was making a mistake by being with her. Ivy didn't belong in his world—a world that was filled with lies and deceit. He had chosen to follow in his father's footsteps and Ivy...she deserved a far better fate than the one his mother was dealt.

She turned in her seat so she could face him directly. "Would it really be so terrible if this deal fell through? Couldn't you move on to the next deal?" She gave a little shrug, "I know it could make you a lot of money but you're already stinking rich. How much more do you need?"

Daniel struggled to find words to explain. It wasn't about the money. Well, it wasn't *just* about the money. "It's the nature of the game—you're only as good as your last deal. If this fails..." He would be a failure. His partners would drop him in a heartbeat. The world he lived in didn't tolerate mistakes, particularly when they cost millions.

She moved to the side of the bed so she could perch beside him and laid a hand on his chest. "It'll happen, Daniel. We'll make it happen."

We. The word was heartening and terrifying all at the same time. But she was right, they *were* a team—for the moment at least. Daniel and Ivy...and Jack. And the frustrating part—the part that made him want to tear the room apart with his bare hands—was that he was useless. At this stage in the game, it all came down to Jack and Ivy and how well they could sell a lie. He would be the first to admit that they had been doing a fantastic job of acting this whole time. So what was it? Why was he stalling?

"It's like Brunelli thinks we're lying," he muttered, dropping his head back against the bedframe in frustration.

Ivy gave him a deadpan look as she stated the obvious. "We *are* lying."

"Yeah, but he doesn't know that."

She raised an eyebrow. "You do realize how ridiculous that logic sounds, don't you?"

Daniel ignored that. He was too busy considering Brunelli's words and actions the night before. "There's more to this than he's letting on. I just wish I knew what his motives were."

"Maybe not everyone has ulterior motives." Now it was his turn to look at her with a raised brow.

She gave in with a sigh. "Okay, fine, believe what you want. But let's look at the silver lining here. You'll have a chance to visit your family. Didn't you say it's been a while since you've visited?"

Daniel's jaw clenched at the mention of them. There was a part of him that wanted to tell her everything. A small, weak part of him craved comfort. But he shoved that voice aside. He was in too deep with Ivy as it was.

"I doubt I'll have time to see them."

She shifted closer on the side of the bed, so soft and delectable and tantalizingly close. "You could always *make* time."

Daniel didn't respond. He wouldn't drag her into his family affairs.

He brought the conversation to an abrupt end when he reached out and tugged her so she toppled onto his chest. She laughed as he wrestled her beneath him, trapping her.

"So I take it you don't want to discuss your family?" she asked.

He leaned in closer and began to nibble on her neck. "I can think of better ways to spend the morning."

Chapter 6

Daniel insisted on driving up to Tuscany, which sounded just fine to Ivy. She had every intention of sightseeing on this trip. The drive should have only taken a few hours but he seemed in no hurry to get there and Ivy and Jack were having so much fun on the road trip—stopping to take pictures, enjoying a leisurely lunch in a quaint town—they were definitely not going to complain.

The closer they got to Tuscany the more tense Daniel seemed to become. Ivy wished Jack was in on their little secret so she could reach a hand out and massage Daniel's stiff shoulders and maybe try to get the truth out of him. It was clear that Brunelli's stall tactics weren't the only thing bothering him about this journey to his homeland.

It was Daniel who insisted that Jack be kept in the dark—not that he didn't trust his business partner, but he felt there was less room for slipups if they kept it to themselves.

Despite the tension in the car, Ivy was enchanted by Tuscany, practically hanging out the window to take in the sweeping views of rolling hills and pastures. "It's so beautiful. You're so lucky you got to spend so much time here."

"Why'd you spend so much time here?" Jack asked from the back seat. Daniel shot her a sidelong glance and she bit her lip.

"I have family around here."

"What? You never told me that." Jack sounded offended in the backseat. He'd lost "shotgun" to Ivy back at the last gas station.

"I wasn't aware I needed to inform you of my ancestry," Daniel said. His voice was droll but there was an edge there that Ivy didn't miss. She would have loved to ask him more but it was clear he didn't want to talk about his family or his memories of the area. Especially not with Jack in the car.

"Was it your mom's side or your dad's? Are they still here?" Jack, who was quickly earning the award for most annoying backseat passenger, didn't seem to pick up on Daniel's not so subtle cues to drop the topic.

"Hey, look over there, it's a vineyard," Ivy said, pointing into the distance with feigned excitement.

"Where?" Jack turned to look where she pointed, despite the fact that they had already passed dozens of vineyards, making Daniel burst out laughing, much to everyone's surprise.

Daniel turned toward Ivy with a grin that took her breath away.

He was handsome in a dangerous sort of way when he was serious— or angry—which was pretty much always. But he was absolutely jaw-droppingly gorgeous when he laughed.

"Very funny," Jack deadpanned. "Don't think you can distract me that easily. I'm finally learning something real about Daniel's life before he became a businessman. This is exciting stuff."

Ivy tended to agree but she knew better than to push. Daniel would open up when he was ready. Or she'd ask him when he was drunk. One or the other.

"It's really not that exciting," Daniel said. "And you should be concerned with Ivy's family, not mine."

Jack turned to her with a look of horror. "Should I be concerned about your family? What's wrong with them?"

Ivy started to laugh but slapped a hand over her mouth when Daniel gave them a warning look. "Brunelli is suspicious, he'll be digging. You two need to be the perfect couple."

Jack leaned forward so he could wrap an arm awkwardly around Ivy's shoulder. "You don't need to worry about us, General. We've got this covered. Don't we Ivy, my love?"

"We're all over it. Go ahead ask me anything. Ask me who Jack brought to his prom."

Daniel rolled his eyes but he was wearing a small smile.

"We're here," Daniel announced.

Ivy nearly mistook Brunelli's house for a palace when they drove up the long, winding driveway. "My goodness, do you think they ever get lost in there?"

"Nah, they've probably had a GPS system installed," Jack said.

Brunelli was hurrying toward them with his arms wide open, as though ready to embrace the car. With his grey hair and twinkling eyes, he looked like everyone's favorite grandfather. Behind him was a small crowd of young women and men. Ivy spotted Angelo in the group and gave him a wave as she exited the car. He grinned from ear to ear before being poked in the ribs by a teenage boy standing next to him.

Brunelli greeted each of them like long lost family and then went on to introduce them to all of his children, grandchildren, nieces and nephews. She lost track of their names somewhere around granddaughter number five but continued to smile and shake their hands as they practiced their English. "Pleee to meeeet you," one of the young girls drawled. Another one of the younger girls slipped her hand into Jack's and gazed up at him in open adoration.

"I think I may have some competition," Ivy said. Brunelli laughed. "Oh, you don't have to worry about Jack. Everyone here knows you two are engaged." He leaned in closer. "Now Danny, on the other hand...." He nodded toward some of the older grandchildren, young women in their early twenties and far too pretty for their own good. They were eyeing Daniel like a piece of filet mignon.

Ivy forced a smile and followed Brunelli as he steered her toward the front door. Angelo had grabbed her bag and was following close behind.

Brunelli put Ivy and Jack in separate rooms in the same wing. He wagged his finger at them. "This is an old-fashioned house—a *traditional* home. You understand, yes? No hanky panky."

They both tried to keep serious faces as they nodded. That would not be a problem. Ivy wasn't sure where Daniel's room was and she figured that might be for the best. It was one thing to deceive Brunelli behind his back; it was quite another to do it in his own home.

Moments after Brunelli left her in her new bedroom, there was a knock at the door. A strikingly beautiful young woman with dark, wavy hair that fell nearly to her waist was standing in her doorway with arms full of towels and bathroom supplies.

"Ciao, I'm Lucia," the eldest granddaughter said, giving Ivy air kisses on both cheeks before moving past her into the room to deposit her load on the bed. "Just in case you don't have something that you need for the toilet." She added with the most adorable Italian accent Ivy had ever heard.

"Thank you, Lucia. That's very kind of you."

The young woman beamed at her and clasped her hands. "We are so excited you're here. Nothing exciting ever happens here but now we have true celebrities."

The girl's almond eyes were wide with excitement.

"We aim to please," Ivy said.

"You'll join us for dinner, no?" Lucia asked.

"Of course, I wouldn't miss it."

"Good. Grandpa has been planning for your arrival for a long time. We are so happy you're finally here."

Lucia left the same way she came in, in a whirlwind of excitement, and Ivy was left to ponder what the young woman had said. How long had Brunelli been planning for them to visit his home? Maybe that had been his plan all along. In that case Daniel should be relieved. It wasn't that Brunelli was suspicious, he just wanted to get to know them better in a more intimate setting. But something about that did not ring true. Why go to such lengths in Rome if he was planning on bringing them here all along? It was almost as though he knew Daniel would need convincing to come out here. But how could he know that?

She heard voices summoning them from the veranda and went off to find the others. She was most likely looking for lies in others because she was lying herself. Talk about paranoia.

* * * *

That night, Brunelli hosted a feast in their honor that would have made the Roman emperors proud. It was unseasonably warm outside so they ate al fresco, with the younger children at one table and the adults at another. The foreign visitors had the seats of honor at the middle of the table. The dinner was filled with talk and laughter as everyone took turns trading stories. Jack, in particular, had everyone in stitches. He was a natural-born comedian. Even Daniel took his turn regaling them with tales of his childhood in the next town over. He went back and forth between Italian and English so even the children could understand. Ivy didn't think she'd ever seen Daniel so relaxed and at ease. She wished the night would never end. The wine flowed freely and by the end of dinner, Ivy was ready collapse from all the food and drink.

She was heading back toward her room, when a hand snaked out of the darkness and yanked her into a room. Before she could utter a cry of alarm, a hand covered her mouth.

"Hello, beautiful." Daniel's low voice sent shivers down her spine. He let his hand drop from her mouth and she sagged against him. "Miss me?"

His lips closed over hers before she could respond. Sweet relief washed over her. Lord, how she'd missed his kiss. She responded hungrily; unable to restrain the instantaneous heat and desire only this man had ever tapped.

He seemed to share the feeling. "God, I've missed you," he whispered as he lifted her into his arms and carried her toward his oversized canopy bed. "I don't know what you've done to me but I can't stop thinking about you."

She thought her heart might burst with pleasure. The words thrilled her nearly as much as the touch of his fingers against her skin. She pulled back an inch, just far enough so she could look him in the eyes.

I love you. The words were there, ready to tumble out of her mouth but she bit them back. It was too soon. And maybe she was wrong; maybe this was just infatuation. A little voice in the back of her mind mocked her as a coward but she shushed it. Instead, she said, "I've missed you too."

His lopsided grin made her smile in return. "It's crazy, isn't it? I just held you this morning. And you've been by my side all day. But I've missed this."

He lay down so his body covered her own and she wrapped her arms around him and pulled him down even closer so she could nibble on his ear, payback for the sweet torture as his hands moved over her breasts.

"It's crazy," she agreed with a sigh.

* * * *

A little while later, she lay curled up against his side, more content than she'd ever been before. "I don't want to go," she whined.

He dropped a kiss on the top of her head and squeezed her tight. "Believe me, I don't want to let you go."

Ivy snuggled up against him. This was it. She'd found her home and it was right here at this man's side. Preferably naked. Was it possible to explode from sheer happiness? Her fingers trailed over his chest and his contented groan made her heart ache with contentment. It wasn't like she'd been completely inexperienced before she met Daniel but in so many ways this felt like her first time. She'd never known being intimate with someone could be like this. So…*intimate.*

She could feel her eyes growing heavy as her breathing slowed and her body seemed to melt into the bed. If she didn't rouse herself soon, she'd be fast asleep in minutes. She sighed in resignation. "I guess I have to go."

"Well, it wouldn't be great for our cover story if anyone caught you sneaking out of my bedroom in the morning," he agreed.

"Yeah yeah."

He tilted her chin up so she was looking at him. "When this is all over, and we're back in New York, I promise you'll not only stay until morning, but I'll wake you with breakfast in bed. How does that sound?"

Ivy's face lit up with a smile but her voice was teasing. "Well that depends. Does breakfast include French toast?"

"But of course."

Ivy pushed herself up and planted a kiss on his lips before grabbing her clothes from the ground. "That French toast better be pretty damn delicious," she added as she walked to the door.

She left with the image of a fantastically sexy and naked Daniel laughing as she shut the door behind her.

Creeping down a stranger's hallway like a burglar hoping desperately that she wasn't caught was not one of Ivy's prouder moments in life. But even her midnight walk of shame couldn't dampen the overwhelming joy she felt when she reached her room and replayed Daniel's remarks.

He cared about her, that much was obvious. This was definitely not some fling, as he'd called it. She grinned at herself in the mirror as she thought of Daniel waking her with breakfast in bed. In his bedroom. In his home. In their future.

She grabbed a pillow and pulled it over her face so no one could hear her squeals of joy.

* * * *

Ivy wasn't the first one at the breakfast table the next morning, but she also wasn't the last—a fact she found vindicating. Daniel, Brunelli, and Jack were all there, as well as most of the younger children and their parents. The teenagers were the last to rise.

If Daniel had harbored any hopes of getting business done on their first day in Tuscany, Brunelli quickly quashed that idea. "I have a bit of a surprise for our visitors today," he announced over a platter of scrumptious looking baked goods. Even Jack looked up from his meal at the proclamation.

"Work?" Daniel suggested mildly.

Brunelli waved away that suggestion with a look of disgust. "There's plenty of time for that. But today, we shall have fun. Show our visitors a good time, eh?"

He looked to Ivy and Jack for approval and found an agreeable audience. "Sounds great," Ivy said.

"So what's the plan?" Jack asked.

"It just so happens that today there will be a festival in town to celebrate the feast day of Saint Castorius. There will be music and food. Our little town puts on quite a celebration."

Ivy clapped her hands in excitement. "How fun! And how lucky that we happened to be here for a festival."

"Not really," Daniel muttered. When she glanced over at him he added, "There are a lot of saints and this town celebrates them all. Every. Single. One."

Brunelli laughed. "It's true. Any excuse to party." He turned to Ivy and Jack. "So what do you say? Shall we celebrate in the true Italian style?"

Ivy and Jack were sold and his grandchildren were just as eager. Lucia, the eldest of the grandchildren by at least ten years agreed to go along to help babysit the youngest. Even Daniel grudgingly agreed to go along.

It only took one hour at the festival before Ivy's stomach was ready to revolt. "Why didn't you tell me there would be so much food?" she groaned. "I wouldn't have eaten such a huge breakfast." Jack's agreement came in the form of an unattractive and absurdly loud belch. "I can't eat another bite."

"But it's all so delicious." Ivy was eyeing a cannoli stand with painful longing.

"Easy, tiger," Daniel said. "Maybe I should have warned you guys about this."

Brunelli was watching them with a look of amusement. "But this is half the fun." He beckoned to them to follow him and his grandchildren to the cannolis but they all declined.

The youngest girl, the one who had been smitten with Jack since he first arrived, tugged on his hand and pointed toward the rides that had been set up on the fairgrounds.

He looked to Daniel and Ivy for help but was met with shrugs. "Okay, fine. One ride. One." He held up a finger to the giggling little girl and she flashed him a toothless grin before dragging him away.

"Oh, poor Jack," Ivy said. She felt a little nauseous just looking at the metal contraptions.

"Poor Jack, but lucky us," Daniel said. He'd moved so he could speak softly into her ear. "Alone at last."

Ivy felt shivers up and down her spine. "And what, pray tell, shall we do to kill the time while Brunelli and his family are away?"

She had to laugh at Daniel's tortured look. "Now, now," she said. "We're on our best behavior, remember?"

"Right. No inappropriate touching. No matter how sexy you may look in that dress."

Ivy felt a flush steal over her skin. "You like it?"

His eyes moved over the thin, simple sheath in appreciation that spoke louder than words. She'd bought the dress in Rome because the salesclerk had told her that the pale blue color and the cut of the fabric was flattering.

"Irresistible," the sales clerk had said. And even though she knew better than to believe a sales clerk who was working on commission, the dress had indeed made her feel feminine and sexy. And yes, she admitted to herself, she had bought it with Daniel in mind, long before he'd kissed her.

She had to stop herself from reaching out and grabbing his hand. They were still in public, even if they did have a brief respite from Brunelli's prying eyes.

"So what shall we do with our precious alone time, considering we can't—you know," Ivy finished with a blush.

"Can't what, Ivy?" he teased. "I have no idea what you mean."

She swatted his arm. "Cut it out."

He pretended to be serious, rocking back on his heels with his hands in his pockets as he feigned deep thought. "Let's see, what could we do together?" He raised his eyebrows. "How about we go for a walk. Burn off some of the food you just scarfed down."

Ivy nodded in agreement. "Great idea."

He led her to a path that ran along the fairgrounds but was behind the vendors and games, off the heavily trafficked main stretch. There they could stroll leisurely without bumping into people left and right.

She took a deep breath and exhaled. "This is nice."

"It is nice, isn't it?" He was watching her with a tender look that made her forget all about the cold, slick tycoon she'd first met. How could she ever have been fooled into thinking this man was heartless?

"So, Miss Sinclair. What do you plan to do with your share of the merger money? Travel the world? Throw some world-class parties? Buy a new wardrobe?" Ivy had to laugh at his game show host impersonation. She was still getting used to this new, playful Daniel and it thrilled her every time he let his guard down around her. Dealing with Daniel was like peeling an onion; there seemed to be no end to his layers.

Ivy pretended to weigh her options. "Oh, I don't know. Maybe buy a yacht?" The thought was so ludicrous, she made herself laugh and he laughed along with her.

"No, seriously," he pressed. "What do you think you'll do? You won't need your hotel job. The world's your oyster."

She glanced over at him in surprise. Somehow she thought he'd known her circumstances. "I'll keep my job, mainly because I like the career path I'm on but also because I'll still need the money."

Now it was his turn to look surprised. "Your portion of the deal isn't enough for you? I would think that would be enough money for a fresh start at the very least."

Ivy hesitated. She wasn't used to discussing her family's troubles with anyone, not even her closest friends. But this was Daniel. She had already given him her heart; it was too late to keep him at arm's length now.

"I'm giving the majority of the money from this deal to my parents."

He stopped in his tracks, the very picture of surprise. "That's very generous of you."

She shrugged. "Not really. They need it more than I do." And then she explained about the hard times her parents had fallen into and how they were close to losing their house.

"So you're handing over all the money you're about to make to save their home?" He didn't sound judgmental but she still felt uncomfortable with the way he was studying her.

She shifted a bit and kept walking so he was forced to follow. "It's my home, too. Why shouldn't I help to keep it?"

"No, of course," he murmured. "I think that's...." She looked over to see him struggling for the right word. "Admirable."

Ivy rolled her eyes at that and they kept walking. "What about you?" she asked. "What are you going to do once this merger is done?"

She tried not to get her hopes up, she really did. But she couldn't pretend that there wasn't a little part of her that was hoping he'd say something romantic. Something about their future together. Instead she got a pragmatic response. "I'll move on to the next deal."

"Oh." She forced a smile to cover her disappointment.

He went on to tell her in great detail about his next project, which involved traveling to the Middle East on a regular basis. She tried not to let her disappointment show. He wouldn't be halfway across the world *all* the time, she reminded herself. And he had promised her breakfast in bed once they returned to New York. She knew it wasn't much of a commitment but it was enough. For now, at least.

Daniel was explaining the trade barriers he would soon be faced with when he was interrupted by a woman's voice. "Danny! Danny!"

The woman who had shouted was Italian, with long, flowing black hair and pretty features. She towed two children along behind her as she made her way to them.

"Who's that?" Ivy glanced over at Daniel when he didn't respond. "Are you all right?" The blood had drawn from his face, leaving him ashen. Like he'd seen a ghost.

THE ACCIDENTAL ENGAGEMENT

"Angela?"

The woman laughed and walked even faster, a broad smile on her face. "Danny, is it you?" The woman ran up to him, ignoring Ivy, and planted two big, wet kisses on his cheeks. She and Daniel held a conversation entirely in Italian and Ivy was left to stand there, watching them in complete bewilderment.

Once Daniel's initial shock passed, he seemed genuinely happy to see the woman before him. Ivy waited for him to introduce her. And waited. And waited. The Italian woman was highly animated, her arms flailing as she rattled off an endless stream of words. Daniel seemed to have forgotten about her.

When at last the two children dragged the woman away, insistently tugging her toward the rides, she kissed Daniel again and called back her goodbyes.

Ivy stood next to Daniel in silence as they watched the woman depart. She glanced at him out of the corner of his eye. He was still staring after the woman even after she disappeared into the crowd.

"Who was that?"

He looked as though he hadn't heard her. Maybe he hadn't. Or maybe he was ignoring her. She didn't want to be jealous, she really didn't. She was not the jealous type. But then, she'd never felt a lot of things until Daniel had come along.

"Shall we head back to meet the others? We wouldn't want them to notice our absence." He was already walking back toward the cannoli stand to meet up with Brunelli and she hurried after him. Once they were surrounded by Brunelli's family she would never get the truth from him.

"Daniel, who was that woman? How do you know her?"

He scanned the crowd for the Brunellis' familiar faces. "Hmm? Oh, she's an old friend."

That was it. That was all she was going to get from him.

* * * *

It was all Daniel could do not to strangle Brunelli when he caught sight of the old man, laughing over his grandchildren's antics. Meddling old fool. He'd known all along that Brunelli was up to something. He knew it was more than just Jack and Ivy's relationship that had led to the invitation to stay with his family in Tuscany. But never in his wildest dreams had he guessed that the true reason was to lure him home.

He studiously ignored Ivy's questioning looks as she all but jogged to keep pace with him. This was not the time to get into it. Not when there was still so much on the line. He'd talked to his fellow investors back in the states that morning and had assured them that the merger was a done deal. But despite his words, everyone knew it wasn't a done deal until the contract was signed.

Daniel could afford to take the loss and his partners could as well, but it would be a serious blow to his career. He had painstakingly built a reputation as the man who got things done in the cutthroat world of venture capital. All it took was one slip, one mistake, and his hard-won reputation would be a memory and everything he'd sacrificed to get to the top would be in vain. He would have to start all over again.

He forced a smile when the old man spotted them and headed toward them with his grandchildren. One of the little ones ran up to them and Ivy caught him in her arms and picked him up. She looked so natural with a child in her arms. She deserved to be with someone who could give her a family. A fresh wave of guilt swept over him; this one having nothing to do with Angela.

Jack walked toward them, his little sidekick running beside him with a grin that spread from ear to ear.

"Looks like someone had fun." Ivy greeted Jack with a kiss on the cheek.

"This one had a blast," Jack said, tousling the little girl's hair. "Uncle Jack, on the other hand, is ready for a nap."

Daniel watched Jack slip an arm around Ivy's shoulders as he pulled her against his side and kissed the top of her head. He should be pleased. They were playing their roles to perfection, just as he'd asked. He turned away from the happy couple.

"I'd better get these little ones back home for a nap or their mother will never forgive me," Brunelli said.

"I think I'm ready for a nap myself," Ivy agreed.

"It's settled then. Let's head back to the villa." Daniel tried his best to keep his tone calm. He could feel Ivy's questioning eyes on him. He'd have to tell her something at some point but not now. Now all he needed was a moment alone with the duplicitous old Italian who was carrying a grandchild in both arms as he led the way to the parking lot.

Daniel rode back with Brunelli, and insisted that Ivy and Jack drive back in another car. He'd suggested that they take their time and do a little sightseeing. A new couple wanting some alone time would only help sell the lie—and it would give Daniel a chance to confront Brunelli on his ulterior motives.

* * * *

Ivy and Jack were quiet as they drove the winding back roads to the villa, killing time so it looked as though they'd snuck off for a little hanky panky, as their host called it.

Jack was driving, which left Ivy free to stare out the window and stew over Daniel's odd behavior. The range of emotions she'd witnessed threw her for a loop. He'd been shocked to see that woman, then genuinely happy, then he'd all but lied to her about who the woman was. But the oddest part of all was his reaction once they'd joined the others. She could have sworn he was furious, but with whom?

"Penny for your thoughts?"

Jack's voice brought Ivy back to the present. "I'm sorry, what were you saying?"

"You look upset. Is everything all right?"

Ivy turned back to look out the window. She hated to lie to her new friend. She tried to stick as close to the truth as possible. "I was just thinking about the festival. Brunelli's grandchildren really are sweet, aren't they?"

Jack nodded. "You're a natural with them."

"I should be. I have four nieces and nephews to practice on."

Jack glanced over at her. "Do you think you'll have kids someday?"

"Of course." The words came out without a second of hesitation. Family had always been the most important thing in her life. It was a given for her that she would have a family of her own.

Jack seemed to be mulling that over. "Good, you'll make a great mother. And Danny is born to be a dad. Although, I think we both know who the disciplinarian will be in your household. Something tells me Daniel will run a tight ship."

Ivy knew she should shut her mouth since no words seemed to be coming out of it, but her jaw was fixed in place. Her mind was reeling. He *knew*? Jack took one look at her expression and burst out laughing. "Oh please. Give me some credit."

"How did you know?"

He rolled his eyes. "The chemistry between you two is through the roof. If you could see the way you look at one another..." he trailed off with a shake of his head.

"Do you think Brunelli knows?"

"No, I think he believes that we're a couple. You're both on your best behavior when he's around."

She let out a sigh of relief. How horrible if they'd gone to all this work only to ruin it in one careless moment. There was so much at stake for everyone involved in this charade. A charade that had been going on for far too long and had gotten way too complicated, as far as she was concerned.

She let her head drop back against the seat. "I hope this deal happens soon."

"You and me both. Lying like this is killing me." Jack's tone was unusually serious. Sometimes she got the feeling that everyone underestimated Jack, including her. He clearly was having just as a hard a time lying to the people he loved as she was.

"Jack, can I ask you something?"

"Of course. Ask away."

"All of these lies we're telling, do you think they're worth it? If it means hurting the people we love?"

He was quiet for a moment. "I'd like to think we're helping the people we love in the long run, at least."

"So the end justifies the means?"

"Something like that." He looked away from the road for a moment to study her expression. "Don't you agree?"

"I guess so." She heaved a sigh as she recalled her last conversation with her parents. They were so strong and proud, even in the face of a foreclosure. When this deal was signed, she could take away all of that stress. "I mean, yes. I do think it's worth it."

"But?"

Ivy struggled to put her finger on what exactly had her so perturbed by Daniel's run-in with that woman. It wasn't jealousy over the woman herself, per se. Although that was definitely part of it. It was the nagging feeling that there was so much more to Daniel that he was keeping from her. Jack was waiting for her response. But what? Why was she having doubts now?

"I know why this deal is so important to me. And I know why you're so invested in this merger—it's a chance to fulfill your dreams. This is the opportunity of a lifetime." Jack's answering grin spoke volumes.

"I guess what I don't quite understand is why this means so much to Daniel. What does he have at stake? Aside from money, I mean."

He shrugged. "This is what he does, it's who he is. His business is his life."

Ivy mulled that over as she watched the scenery slip past her window. Was he really the single-minded businessman everyone believed him to be? She had a flash of his grin when he woke her with kisses and saw the tender look in his eyes when he held her in his arms.

"Do you really believe that?"

"That he's all business? Yeah. I mean, I've never once heard him talk about friends or family or anything other than the merger, for that matter."

Ivy frowned as she stared out the window. She tried to remember any time Daniel had mentioned anything other than business. Even when the two of them were alone and in the most intimate setting imaginable, he never spoke about himself or his life outside of the company. Every time she brought it up, he steered the conversation back to her, asking her about her family, her friends. She wracked her brain trying to remember a time when he'd mentioned anything personal. Surely he must have told her about *something*.

At Ivy's silence, he hurried on. "Not that that's a bad thing. That's why I like working with him. It's not personal for Daniel."

Ivy looked at him in disbelief. "And you're saying that's a good thing?"

Jack's fingers tapped the steering wheel and there was a long pause before he spoke. "I made the mistake before of mixing my personal life with business. My first investors were was also my brother and my so-called best friend."

She studied his clenched jaw. "I take it he's not your best friend anymore?"

Jack gave her a rueful smile. "No. We're not even on speaking terms any more. I trusted him because of our friendship and my brother…. He made the colossal mistake of trusting me. Like the idiot I am, I didn't get a lawyer of my own to read through all of the papers my friend had me sign."

He shook his head in disgust and she winced in sympathy. "What happened?"

"Let's just say that in the end, all of my hard work ended up becoming his property and I was left with next to nothing."

"Nothing except for your name and reputation for genius," she reminded him.

He smiled over at her but the smile didn't reach his eyes. "Exactly. That much at least was enough to get me meetings with new investors. But the world of venture capitalism is cutthroat. It's hard to know who to trust."

"But you trust Daniel," she said.

He looked surprised. Almost offended. "Of course. But that's my point. I trust Daniel because it's all about the deal with him. There's nothing personal about it."

She smiled over at Jack, breaking the serious mood. "I don't think that's true at all. You wouldn't trust him if you didn't believe he was just as invested as you are. If you didn't believe that he was honest and had integrity and was looking out for your best interests."

Jack smiled over at her. "You really are smitten, aren't you?"

Ivy grimaced. "Is it that obvious?"

"Well, let's just say, he's lucky to have found a woman who can see the best qualities in him despite his best efforts to keep them hidden."

Ivy rolled her eyes. "He's not that bad. I know he can act like a tin man but he does have a heart you know."

"If you say so. You know him better than I do." He wriggled his eyebrows suggestively. "You know him far more intimately, if you know what I mean."

Ivy laughed and looked pointedly at her watch. "Have we stayed away long enough yet? I'm beginning to tire of all this hanky panky."

Jack let out a snort of laughter and picked up the speed. "Do you mind if I just drop you off? Brunelli's son told me he'd give me a tour of the plant."

He looked as excited as a little kid at Christmas. "Go nuts. I can occupy myself for an afternoon."

Chapter 7

The villa was oddly quiet and empty with the little ones sleeping. She wasn't sure where the other grown ups were. Maybe they needed a nap even more than the kids. She wandered from one room to another, unsure of what to do with herself. There must be a library around somewhere.

She was headed in a direction that she hoped led to a library when she heard their voices. Or rather, when she heard Daniel. She'd never heard him raise his voice before and the sound of his fury was frightening.

"You have gone too far, Gianni. I mean it."

She couldn't make out Brunelli's words but he sounded like he was trying to appease him.

"I don't care how great your intentions were, you had no right to interfere with my family. How long have you been friends with my grandfather? Because I don't remember you being around when I was a kid."

Again there was a soft murmur, Brunelli trying to calm him down, she imagined, but Daniel only got louder.

"If he told you everything, he must have told you about the ultimatum he gave me and how I chose to leave him and the family. I made my decision, Brunelli. What's done is done."

She heard a door slam and footsteps heading toward the veranda. Ivy hesitated for a moment before following. She found Daniel alone out back, staring out at the rolling hills that seemed to go on forever.

"Daniel?"

He didn't answer. She walked up behind him and laid a hand on his back. "Go back inside, Ivy." His voice was gruff.

She stayed where she was. "What happened?"

"I mean it, Ivy. If Brunelli comes out here and finds us together like this…."

Ivy let out an exasperated sigh. "Just forget about the precious deal for one minute and tell me what's going on. Maybe I can help."

He spun around so quickly, her hand was knocked aside. "You know how you can help? You can go back inside and stay away from me. The only reason you're here is to play your role. That's it. If you can't do that one simple task—" He cut himself off with a curse.

Tears pricked the back of her eyes but she blinked them back. He was emotional, he was venting. She could take it.

He turned his back again and raked a hand through his hair. "Goddammit, Ivy."

She knew there was every chance that Brunelli or one of his brood would walk out at any moment. "Come on," she said. "Let's go for a walk."

* * * *

Daniel felt like the worst kind of heel. He tried to apologize for his outburst but she waved him off. She grabbed his hand and led him down a path that veered away from the main house. "Where are we going?"

"Somewhere we can talk without interruption." Despite her size, she had the air of a commander and he brooked no argument as he followed her into a thicket of tall trees. There was a clearing in the middle with some large boulders. She perched atop one and patted the spot next to her.

He sat down and let his head drop into his hands. She didn't push him but he knew she was waiting for him to speak. "He wants me to reconcile with my family." He looked up then and saw her watching him with concern. And something more.

Alarm bells went off. He was entering into dangerous territory—or maybe he'd entered that dangerous territory the moment he'd kissed her in the elevator. The look she was giving him screamed commitment and future. Damn it, why had he given in to temptation? He should never have strayed from the jaded, worldly women of his set. Now this beautiful, sweet woman was going to get hurt and it was his fault.

She was waiting for him to continue and he found that he actually wanted to tell her the whole story. He *needed* to tell her. The time would come for him to put an end to their tryst—as soon as the deal was done and the engagement was called off, he would end their affair. There was no room for a woman like her in his life—not in the long run. In the meantime, while she was still in his life, he was compelled to be honest with her.

"My father was a hard man. Not cruel, just not capable of the kind of love my mother needed. He was always off traveling for business. In his defense, it was his way of proving he cared. He did it all for us. He built an empire and he paid for us to have everything we could dream of."

He gave her a rueful look. "All my mother wanted was a husband and a father for her child and that was the only thing he couldn't give her."

Ivy looked so hurt on his behalf, he had to look away.

"She was lonely, stuck at home with just a small child for company, so we began to take more and more trips to Italy so she could spend time with her family. They took us in with open arms and helped to raise me."

Pain stabbed his chest as he forced away a wave of nostalgia that had threatened to drown him ever since he'd arrived in Tuscany. This place had been his own personal heaven when he was young. Before he'd left it all behind.

"I was very close with my grandfather in particular. He filled the role that my own father never could."

She slipped her hand into his and he gave it a squeeze.

"But then my mother died. It happened when I was away at college. She got sick. She had cancer. They caught it too late and she went quickly."

He paused to take a deep breath. His voice sounded wooden and stilted even to him. It occurred to him that this was the first time he had ever told anyone about his mother's death. He looked over to see Ivy listening intently, tears glistening in her eyes. She was crying over a woman she'd never even met.

"I'm so sorry, Daniel."

He nodded and wrapped an arm around her shoulders. She burrowed into his side, fitting perfectly as though her body had been designed to mold against his.

"What happened between you and your family?"

"My father was devastated when she died. Despite everything, he loved her. He just wasn't capable of being the type of man that she needed."

He could feel Ivy nod in understanding. "I think he wanted to make it up to me—make up for all the years he hadn't been around. Make up for the fact that I'd lost my mother. So he invited me into his business. He wanted to train me to be his right-hand man and run the company after he was gone."

"And your grandfather didn't want that?"

Daniel's laugh came out harsher than he intended. "That's putting it mildly. My grandfather was—*is*—a stubborn man and he hated my father for the way he failed my mother. He blamed him for every sadness in her life."

He shrugged. "I was angry at him too, I guess. But I was also desperate to forge some sort of connection with my father. I'd spent my whole childhood hoping that he would notice me, that he would pay attention. So when he finally did—I couldn't say no."

There was a brief silence and he could hear crickets in the distance. "I haven't seen my family since."

"Oh Daniel." Ivy wrapped her arms around him and held on tight. The pain in his chest eased slightly.

He stroked her hair and let himself remember the days when these hills had been his own personal playground. This place had been paradise until his mother died. And then it was just a painful reminder. The years had helped to buffer the grief but it was still there beneath the surface.

"Brunelli, the meddling old fool, is friends with my grandfather. Turns out his real motive for getting us out here was to help us reconcile."

"How do you know?"

"Angela, the woman who ran over to us at the festival?" He saw Ivy nod out of the corner of his eye. "She's my cousin. We were best friends when we were young. She told me that they were throwing a party for my grandfather's birthday. The whole family is here. She let it slip that they had all been holding out hope that I would arrive and make amends with the old man."

Daniel felt a bitter taste in the back of his mouth. "Apparently my grandfather's best friend, Brunelli, promised them that he would deliver the prodigal grandson."

"Is that what your grandfather wants?"

Daniel frowned. "Brunelli said he did. He said he's getting old and wants to make peace before it's too late." He shook his head. "But that doesn't sound like him."

Despite all the years that had passed, he could still see the betrayal in the old man's eyes the last time they'd met. The day his grandfather had kicked him out of his home and told him never to return.

"What about the rest of your family? The people who helped to raise you?"

He smiled at the memory of his aunts and uncles chasing after him. "I would love to see them. But I can't imagine they'd want to see me. They wouldn't like what they find."

Ivy pushed herself away and turned to look at him. "What do you mean?"

He looked into that sweetly innocent face. She might as well hear the truth sooner rather than later. "They all hated my father—hated the type of man he was. And that's who I've become. I am my father's son."

He'd said it. She should know what she had gotten herself into.

They sat in silence for a while, each lost in thought. Daniel found himself wondering if what he'd said had gotten through to her. He hoped so, for her sake. Her eyes needed to be opened. He never had been, and never would be, long-term commitment material. He glanced down at the top of her auburn head and for one moment had a flash of a possible future—he saw her sitting there with a belly round with his child; he had a flash of painting a nursery together in a home of their own.

Good God, snap out of it. That was not the life for him. That decision had been made years ago and he was happy with his choice. He'd learned the hard way that, despite best intentions, men like Daniel and his father weren't cut out to be family men. He wouldn't do to any woman or child what his father had done to them. Guilt at his selfishness these last few days ate at him, but it was too late now. Daniel couldn't undo what had already happened. She would be hurt when he ended it but it would be for her own good.

Ivy had apparently also been coming to a conclusion of her own. "You should go to him." Before he could open his mouth to respond she pushed on. "He's getting older and he may not have much time left. He's reaching out and making the first move, something that can't be easy if he's as stubborn as you say."

She had a point there. He was having a hard time imagining his grandfather giving in. Maybe he was getting softer in his old age.

"Unless Brunelli's lying," he said. "Angela never mentioned anything about grandfather wanting to see me. Maybe that's just another part of Brunelli's lies."

Ivy's voice was quiet. "You won't always have this opportunity. Do you really want to live with the regret of knowing you could have given him peace but didn't because you were too stubborn?"

Her words hit home. Maybe he'd inherited something from his mother's side after all—their stubbornness. He sighed and kissed the top of her head. "Maybe you're right."

"I *know* I'm right." He laughed at her smug look. "I may not be winning any daughter of the year contests at the moment, you know with my big fat lies and all—but I do know this—where there is love there is forgiveness. Everyone deserves a second chance."

Her gaze was filled with such guilelessness. She was such an innocent in so many ways. She actually did believe that love conquered all. And the way she was looking at him at that moment....

Oh no. Oh hell. Oh hell no.

He dropped the arm that was around her and tried to inch away a bit. What had he done? This was supposed to be a fun little tryst. She wasn't supposed to fall in love with him. He'd known she was going to get hurt but he never intended to break an innocent girl's heart. He had to put an end to this.

They heard voices coming from further down the path and he stood, tugging her to her feet. "Come on, let's get out of here before anyone sees us together."

* * * *

Ivy overslept. By the time she wandered into the kitchen the next morning, she learned that everyone else had already eaten and were going about their day. Since she had nothing to do while the others worked, she took her coffee out to the veranda to enjoy the peace and quiet. She breathed in the fresh, fragrant air. She would miss this when she was back in her noisy Brooklyn studio.

She was pondering the feasibility of creating a "Tuscany Hills" air freshener when Brunelli came out to join her. "Ah, you've found my favorite spot, I see." He pulled up a cushioned chair beside her and together they looked out over the land.

"Where's your husband-to-be this morning?"

She glanced over in surprise. "I thought he was with you at the office."

He shook his head. "I didn't go into work this morning. I took Daniel over to see his family."

She couldn't hide her shock. "He decided to go?"

Brunelli smiled. "He did. He finally came to his senses. I think I have you to thank for that." She felt her cheeks flush with pleasure and turned her face away. She didn't know what Daniel had told him about their conversation and didn't want to give herself away.

"How did it go? With his family, I mean."

Brunelli grinned from ear to ear. "It couldn't have gone better. He was welcomed into the fold like the prodigal son that he is."

Ivy was smiling now, too, unable to hide her excitement. "And his grandfather?"

"Old Maurice burst into tears at the sight of him and embraced him." He shook his head, his own eyes glistening at the memory. "Italian men, especially in Daniel's family, they can be so stubborn, so thick-headed. They'd cut off their nose to spite their face, that's the saying, yes?"

Ivy nodded and laughed. "That's the saying."

"I should know," he added. "I am just as stubborn. That's how Maurice and I came to be friends, you know. After he lost Daniel…after he pushed him away…he and I became close. He knew I could understand because I too made mistakes with my family. I let pride get in the way…" his voice trailed off and the sad expression on his face made him seem older than his age. "I lost my chance to make things right but Maurice….it wasn't too late for him." He heaved a sigh and added, "Sometimes it takes an old meddling fool like me to help them see what's right in front of their faces."

Ivy looked at him with narrowed eyes. The crafty old devil had been playing them all along. "That was awfully tricky of you, using the merger to get Daniel out here."

Brunelli took a sip of his coffee and stared straight ahead, a little grin the only acknowledgement of his deception.

Ivy laughed and leaned back in her seat. "And here I thought you wanted us out here to make sure Jack and I are really in love." She surprised herself when the words slipped out of her mouth but Brunelli threw his head back and laughed.

"That's what I like about you, Ivy. You're so honest."

Guilt stabbed her like a knife. She had been lying to this man since the moment they'd first met, not to mention everyone she loved.

"And you're right. That was part of the reason I wanted you all out here," he admitted.

And? She wanted to say. *Are you convinced? Can we finally end this silly game?*

She held her tongue and sipped her coffee instead.

"Doesn't it bother you?" At her questioning look, he explained. "Doesn't it bother you that he is using you and your love for a business deal?"

He was talking about Jack, of course, but Ivy found herself asking the same question about Daniel. Nerves made her stomach churn. How far would he go? How far would he push her to make this deal happen? She tilted her head to the side and tried to be as honest as possible. "Not really. This deal means a lot to him. And to Daniel, too. I'll do whatever I can to help make it a reality."

She'd answered truthfully but knew she was lying by omission by leaving out some key facts. For example, the fact that coming here meant she was going to be financially stable and able to save her parents' house didn't hurt either.

He seemed to be studying her and she tried her best not to give anything away. Suddenly she wished she'd taken those acting lessons her sister had always wanted.

"You are more understanding than most. But I appreciate you accommodating an old man."

Ivy raised a brow. "This whole thing…it's a bit old-fashioned, don't you think?"

He laughed again. "You say 'old-fashioned', I say 'wise.' I put a lot of faith in family values." He gestured around him. "The love that comes with family, that is everything. I've been approached by countless corporations and conglomerations, all trying to make a deal with me. They've all offered plenty of money and resources but they all lacked one thing." He tapped a hand against his heart. "They didn't have *soul*. They didn't have true passion for their projects or for their employees."

"And you think the only way someone can have this…*passion*, is to be in love?"

His smile was warm and kind and she was reminded that this was a man who'd raised a brood of children and even more grandchildren. "The kind of love I'm talking about means placing people above profit. It means loving someone else more than yourself. It's not necessarily a love between two married people. However I do believe that the sort of love I'm talking about cannot be understood until it is experienced." His next words surprised her. "Daniel, now there is a man who is capable of great love."

Ivy shot the older man a sidelong look. "And Jack?"

He took another sip. "I have watched Jack at work—it is clear that he has passion for his work." She noted his vague answer; he was still not convinced that Jack was in love with her. What on earth would it take with this man?

* * * *

Daniel sipped his coffee on the back porch of a house he used to call home. His reunion with his family had gone remarkably well but it had been emotionally exhausting. He couldn't believe the change in his grandfather. He was an old man now. He had known that before he arrived, obviously, but seeing the frail man with his own eyes had still been disconcerting. And it wasn't only his appearance that had changed. The once rigid and stubborn man had actually apologized to Daniel for the things he'd said all those years ago. He still couldn't believe it.

Angela came out to join him, plopping down with a sigh of exhaustion. "The kids are finally asleep."

"Good, then you can join me for a nightcap."

She nodded to the coffee in his hand. "I'm surprised you didn't opt for something stronger after the day you've had."

Daniel laughed. She had a point. After the initial emotional reunion with his grandfather, he had been enveloped into the animated and loud family reunion. He'd seen relatives he'd spent countless hours with and met many new additions to the family. It seemed all of his cousins had settled down and were now the proud parents of a small army of children.

"So, who was that woman you were with at the festival?"

Uh oh. Here it comes. He hadn't missed the looks his family had exchanged when they discovered that he was single and childless—a fate worse than death in this family.

There it was again. The image he'd had the other day of Ivy round with child. Ivy walking down the aisle. Ivy growing old at his side.

Snap out of it, Danny boy. She deserves better.

"She's nobody, just someone I work with." He hadn't meant to sound so defensive. He offered a small smile. "No setups, I'm begging you. Take my word for it when I tell you I am not marriage material."

Angela feigned innocence. "Who said anything about marriage?" She caught his eye and they both burst out laughing. "Okay, okay. Maria, Juliette, and I may have come up with a few available women we'd like you to meet—I'm serious, stop laughing."

Daniel shook his head. "You guys are too much. I've only been here a few hours and already you're trying to boss me around. Just like old times."

Angela pretended to be hurt. "Are you calling me bossy?"

Daniel looked at her in disbelief.

"Okay, fine. Maybe I'm a little bossy. You would be too if you were the oldest of five."

"Touché."

They sipped their drinks in silence for a few moments, enjoying the fresh night air before Angela picked up where she'd left off. "So, seriously. What's the deal with you and that woman?"

Daniel sighed and put down his coffee cup. She wouldn't stop until he spilled. "It's complicated. I'd rather not talk about it."

Angela made a snorting noise and waved away his protest. "That excuse might work on your employees but it won't work with your family."

When he still didn't speak, she kept pestering. "Is she your girlfriend?"

"No," he said quickly. Too quickly.

Her eyes searched his face. "Does she know that she's not your girlfriend?"

Guilt swirled in his stomach. Guilt and something else he couldn't name. Disappointment maybe. Or regret. He didn't want to be having this conversation. "Why would you think that?"

"Because I'm a *woman*," she said as though that answered everything. She rolled her eyes at Daniel's blank look. "I can tell when another woman is in love."

Love. The word hit Daniel like a punch in the gut. He'd suspected it from the way she looked at him, the way her eyes lit up when he entered a room. But he had hoped he was wrong. Hoped maybe she was harboring a schoolgirl's crush.

How had he gotten himself into this? She was everything he'd always avoided in women. And now he'd gone and done the unthinkable. He was going to break an innocent woman's heart. Despite all of his precautions, he was still no better than his father after all.

Angela had been watching him and her voice lost all of its mockery and flippancy. She talked to him like she did one of her children, like a patient mother. "You care about her too," she said.

He didn't respond because he didn't have to. It wasn't a question and there was no point denying it. Yes, he cared. Of course he cared. And that was why he had to keep his distance.

Too little too late. Where had that resolve been a week ago? It was too late to undo what he'd already done, but from here on out he would create distance. He would back away and when the time was right, he would end it for good. A clean break. She was young and beautiful. She'd find someone else, someone who could help her to move on.

He slammed his coffee cup down with such force the table shook and Angela sat up with a start. "Sorry," he muttered.

"Talk to me, Danny. If you care about her and she's clearly smitten with you—what's the hold up?"

He stared at her in disbelief. He'd thought Angela would understand. She'd been there for every missed birthday, every heartbreaking disappointment. She'd watched by his side as his mother hid her tears every time. "You of all people should know what would happen to this girl if we actually stayed together."

He sighed in exasperation at her confused look. "You saw what life was like for my mother. And for me. I couldn't put any woman through that, especially not Ivy."

Her eyes widened in understanding. "You don't really believe that's true? You're nothing at all like your father."

Daniel squashed a wave of anger. "I'm exactly like him. I made my decision to follow in his footsteps a long time ago and I haven't looked back."

Angela pursed her lips. It was clear she wanted to debate the issue further but was holding herself back.

"Trust me, Angela. If you knew Ivy, you wouldn't wish that for her either."

"Have you asked her what she wants in all of this? Because it sounds like you've made up your mind for both of you."

"She's young and naïve. She'll thank me for it one day." One day when she was happily married to some other man. There was a loud cracking sound when he accidentally snapped off the handle of his mug. "Stupid piece of...."

He looked up to see Angela smothering a laugh at his expense.

* * * *

Ivy was dying for a moment alone with Daniel. He hadn't returned to the villa for dinner and she hadn't seen him before everyone retired to their bedrooms. She was hoping he'd slip into her room if he got in late, but she had no late night visits either. The next morning she sought him out so she could hear every detail of the reunion. Maybe he'd thought to take pictures. Probably not.

Daniel finally made an appearance during breakfast. She tried to catch his eye when the others were talking but he looked distracted. Maybe the reunion hadn't gone as well as Brunelli thought or maybe they'd gotten into a huge fight after he left. Ivy played with the pastry on her plate and silently urged everyone to leave them alone. Just for two minutes, she begged telepathically. But no such luck. She was forced to smile and play lovebirds with Jack until he left for the office with Brunelli's son and then Daniel and Brunelli went off to discuss business.

She was in the living room, watching some of the younger children play when Brunelli and Daniel walked into the room. It was Brunelli who finally gave her the golden opportunity.

"Poor Ivy is stuck inside all day, waiting around for Jack." He made a tsking noise. "Daniel, you know your way around town, no? Take this poor girl out and show her a good time, for heaven's sake."

Ivy clapped her hands in excitement. She was desperate for time alone with Daniel but she still had to play the role. "Don't you want to come? And what about the children?"

He made a shooing motion with his hands. "You both look like you need some sunshine and fresh air. Go, go. No arguments."

And so Ivy found herself alone at last with Daniel. "First thing's first." She scooted across the middle seat and wrapped an arm around his neck, pulling him in for a kiss. He pulled back a little too quickly and put the car in gear. "We'd better keep moving. I wouldn't put it past Brunelli to have spies watching us."

Ivy gave him a questioning look but let it go. "So, tell me everything. I'm dying to hear how it went."

He smiled at her and she felt a chill run down her spine. There it was. There was that dreaded, slick smile she despised. She hadn't seen that since they slept together.

Shaking off a sense of foreboding, Ivy paid attention as he described the same scene that Brunelli had told her about and went on to give her the gist of his conversation with his grandfather. "We both decided to put the past behind us. He's in poor health and he wants to put away the grudges and misunderstandings and I told him that I'd like very much to have him back in my life."

Ivy reached over to squeeze his arm. "I'm so happy for you, Daniel. "

"I know I have you to thank. Well, you and Brunelli."

"Speaking of Brunelli...." Ivy took a deep breath and recounted the conversation from the other morning. When she was finished, his jaw was clenched.

"Dammit." He pounded a fist against the steering wheel, causing Ivy to jump.

"Do you think he suspects something? Between us, I mean?"

He shook his head. "I don't know. But clearly he's still not sold on you and Jack. Where is he, anyway? The whole point of coming up here is so Brunelli can see the two of you together."

"He's been working."

"Well, he can work all he wants once this deal is signed. Until then, his only job is to convince Brunelli he's a man in love. And a man in love wouldn't choose to work over spending time with his fiancée during her first trip to Tuscany."

Ivy was watching his profile closely. What had happened between yesterday and today?

The rest of the afternoon was a miserable failure as far as Ivy was concerned. She'd been so looking forward to an afternoon alone with Daniel and instead she found herself walking beside a bored tour guide.

"To the left is the first church built in the town, I believe it dates back to the Renaissance."

She was only half listening. At one point she tried to ask him about his change of behavior but he played dumb and said he didn't know what she was talking about.

When he wasn't explaining the history of the town, he was strategizing over how best to sell Ivy and Jack as a couple. After lunch he scrutinized the way they greeted each other, their pet names and how often they held hands. "There's not enough PDA between you two, that's definitely a problem."

She threw her hands in the air in annoyance. "What do you want me to do, throw myself on top of him every time he walks into the room? Shove my tongue down his throat at dinner?"

Daniel cast her a warning look. "This isn't funny, Ivy. I've got everything on the line here. And so does Jack. And so do you, for that matter. It's time you take this seriously."

Ivy had to bit her tongue to keep from sticking it out at him like a child. "You think I'm not taking this seriously? I've put my life on hold and am lying to everyone I know. Do you know my parents were asked to be on a talk show to discuss my upbringing? Everyone wants the story of my life and it's one big lie. Don't tell me I'm not taking it seriously."

Ivy tried to get it out of him. "What is this really about?"

"What do you mean?"

"I mean, who are you? You're not the same guy you have been for the past few days. What's changed?"

He paused while walking and gave her a serious look. "Get used to it, Ivy. This is the real me. I don't know what you think was going on but I'm here for one reason and one reason only. Got it?"

Ivy's breath caught in her throat at his tone. She tried to let it go. She tried to focus on the buildings he was showing her and give them both some time to cool off. She would wait and talk to him when she was calm and collected. It was a lovely thought.

"What happened yesterday?"

He turned to her, looking slightly surprised to find her still walking by his side. "I already told you. I had a nice reunion with my family. Are you ready to head back to the villa yet?"

She was a dog with a bone. No matter how much she wished she could be sensible and let the conversation lie, her mouth had other ideas. "Why are you being such a jerk?"

The look he gave her was that of an overly patient uncle. "I have no idea what you're talking about, Ivy. If I've offended you in some way, I apologize." He started to walk away but she stopped him by stepping directly into his path. "Fine. Don't tell me what happened. But don't try to deny that something is different between us. You're back to being... back to being...."

His cool smile was the last straw.

She jabbed a finger at his chest. "There it is. That smile. I *hate* that smile."

She saw a muscle in his jaw twitch. There. At least she was getting some sort of reaction.

"I don't know what's going on with you but I don't understand how you can go from being a kind, attentive, loving—" She almost said boyfriend before she stopped herself. Now was not the time to define their relationship, not when he was pushing her away.

She lowered her voice so the passersby on the street couldn't hear. "You slept with me. You made love to me just two nights ago."

He pulled her off of the sidewalk where they were starting to garner attention and into a small alley beside a church. When he spoke, his voice was cold and detached. "What do you want from me?"

His cold tone was a knife in her gut. She drew back, stunned by the stranger who stood before her. This man was nothing like the Daniel she had come to know. He wasn't even the formal businessman she had originally met. The man who stood before her was a stranger.

"I mean it, Ivy. What do you want?"

"I don't know what you mean."

His tone was condescending. "I think you do. This is about us, isn't it? About our little affair?" He waved his hand in the air dismissively.

Ivy blinked at him in surprise. He was being cruel. And it was intentional.

"I thought I made myself very clear from the very beginning, my dear. I told you from the start that I wouldn't let some fling stand in the way of this deal. I meant what I said. Now, I don't know what sort of childish notions you've gotten into your head but it's time you grow up."

Ivy's head snapped back as though he'd slapped her across the face.

"Grow up?" she echoed stupidly.

He rubbed a hand across his eyes as though he was dealing with a petulant child. "I should have known you couldn't handle a casual affair." He let out weary sigh. "Did you really think I would give everything up for you? That I would let a little tryst get in the way of a deal that has been two years in the making?"

She didn't know how to respond. "I—I didn't expect you to give up anything for me." She waited for him to continue, to explain what had brought this on. But instead he turned away from her and started walking away.

"Don't forget why you're here, Ivy. Nothing else matters."

* * * *

The car was filled with tense silence on the way back to the villa. Once there, Ivy escaped to her room where she had plenty of time to replay the events of the afternoon. It wasn't long before anger replaced hurt and there were a million things Ivy wished she'd said. A million things she *needed* to say.

She went off in search of him, down the many hallways and into empty rooms but Daniel was nowhere to be found. The more she looked, the angrier she became until, by the time she found him and Lucia alone together in Brunelli's study, she was ready to scream.

They both looked up in surprise when she stormed in and Ivy caught herself just in time before she started in on a rampage.

"Oh, hi Ivy," Lucia said. The younger, glamorously gorgeous woman was beaming at her and in that moment, Ivy knew what jealousy was.

Daniel was lounging beside her, looking at pictures on her phone, by the looks of it—and looking like a man without a care in the world. Meanwhile she'd been stewing and obsessing and boiling over with rage.

"Am I interrupting something?" she asked. She was looking at Daniel, only at Daniel, but it was Lucia who spoke.

"Nothing important. Danny just wanted to see some pictures of my designs. I'm studying to be a fashion designer."

Ivy turned to Daniel with a look of surprise. "I had no idea you were interested in fashion design."

The look in his eyes was so cold, so distant; it turned her hot fury into bone-chilling horror. His detachment was a dagger in her heart. He ignored her completely and turned to Lucia with that dazzling smile that she loved so much.

"Your designs are amazing, my dear. You have true talent."

Lucia basked in his praise and started to put her phone away. "I'm so glad you think so. Now come, both of you, Grandpa will kill us if we're late to dinner."

Ivy tried her best to put on a happy face over dinner that night but was eternally grateful to have the ever-smiling Jack at her side to keep the conversation flowing. She was too distracted by watching Daniel flirt with Lucia at the other end of the table. They were speaking Italian but she could interpret high-pitched giggles and whispered asides with no help from a translator.

She tried to focus on the conversation that Jack was having with Brunelli but all she could think of was what she should have said. What she should have done. Of all times for her big mouth to suddenly take a vacation, it had to be this afternoon when the man she'd been intimate with—the man she thought she loved—all but accused her of being a pathetic child with a crush.

She felt red-hot fury course through her body every time she remembered his cruel words.

"Really, Brunelli, your home and this village—it may be the most beautiful place on earth," Jack was saying. The younger family members all cheered this declaration and Brunelli grinned. "I'm so glad you like it here. And what about you, my dear?" he asked Ivy.

She turned her attention away from Daniel. "I adore it," she said with all honesty. "Your home, the town, this landscape…it's pure magic."

"It's very romantic, no?"

Ivy and Jack both agreed that it was indeed romantic.

"Good. " Brunelli clapped his hands as though a deal had been struck. "Then it is official. You shall marry here."

Ivy knew her jaw was gaping unattractively but couldn't seem to close it. Jack recovered first. "Excuse me?"

"We will host your marriage ceremony here." And then for the final kicker, "In two days."

"B-but, we can't," Ivy stammered.

"Isn't that a bit quick?" Jack asked.

"Why not?" All eyes turned to Daniel. "I think it's a fantastic idea."

Ice water rushed through Ivy's veins. This could not be happening. She turned to Jack, who looked just as horrified by the sudden turn of events. Daniel on the other hand seemed completely unfazed. She couldn't seem to tear her eyes away from his face, from those cold, unfeeling eyes. What had happened to him? What had happened to *them*?

Daniel put down his fork and leaned back in his chair. "I think it's a terrific idea," he repeated.

Brunelli looked overwhelmed with excitement. "Yes, yes. It's been too long since we've had a celebration in this household. It will be perfect."

Ivy and Jack open their mouths to interrupt but he cut them off. "Don't worry about a thing. My family and I will take care of everything. Every detail will be accounted for. It will be perfection."

He launched into conversation with his daughters and nieces who seemed equally enthusiastic about the plan.

She and Jack shared a look of horror. This was spinning out of control. Were they really discussing marriage? As in *marriage*?

She shot Daniel a pleading look but it went unanswered. Whether he was pointedly ignoring her or was truly fascinated by the wedding planning going on around him was unclear. Rage began to replace her initial shock. How could he go along with this? How could he take Brunelli's side? Didn't it bother him at all that she would be marrying another man?

Chapter 8

"No!"

All eyes turned to Ivy with varying shades of shock. All but Daniel. He was glaring at her like she was some disobedient child.

This could not be happening.

She turned to Jack who tried to intervene. "I think what Ivy means is, we have a plan of our own for the wedding and—"

"But Ivy told me you two haven't started planning yet," Lucia interrupted. All sweetness and wide eyed, Ivy had an urge to strangle her. It was true, the two women had been chatting over breakfast a few days before and the younger woman kept asking her questions about the wedding, where it would be, how many guests, what kind of flowers… Ivy had thought the safest answer would be 'we haven't even begun to think about it.'

She was wrong.

Jack turned to her with a look of panic that she was sure mirrored her own.

Ivy tried in vain to give reasons why a wedding in Tuscany would not be possible. Her family, first and foremost—Brunelli rushed to assure her that he would fly them all over here on his private jet. But what about her friends? He laughed, had she not heard the part about the private jet?

Jack tried, too, but all of their worries and concerns were waved away and their excuses to put off the wedding grew more and more absurd. Ivy was ready to kick Daniel she was so furious with him. All throughout the conversation, rather than taking their side, he did everything in his power to help convince them that Brunelli was right. He was all for the wedding.

She could see his mind ticking away; if they married, then and there, Brunelli would have absolutely no room left to procrastinate. It would be a done deal. For one paranoid moment she was convinced that he and Brunelli had concocted this scheme together. But she couldn't bear the thought that he would plot against her or Jack like that. Even if he had been a jerk that afternoon, she still couldn't bring herself to believe he'd go behind their backs.

Ivy made her excuses early; telling the two puppet masters that she had a lot to think over. It wasn't long before there was a knock on her bedroom door. She knew who it would be before she opened the door.

"Can I come in?" Daniel asked.

Ivy's lips were compressed into a thin line. She scanned the hallway in an exaggerated motion. "Aren't you worried one of the Brunellis will catch you speaking with me?"

He pushed past her. "Listen, I know you're upset—"

"Oh, really? How perceptive of you, Sherlock Holmes."

"There's no need to be snarky." His condescending tone only added fuel to her fire.

"Don't you dare tell me how to behave. Not here in my bedroom. You already pull all the strings out there." She jabbed a finger toward the hallway. "But in here I am my own woman."

He folded his arms and eyed her like she was a troublesome student. "This is the only way to finish this deal. Once it's done, we'll sign the deal and you can have the marriage annulled. Everyone will go their separate ways. No harm, no foul."

She was staring at him in horror. "Is that what a wedding means to you? That's what marriage is for you? A means to an end?" She was choking on pent up tears but refused to let him see her cry. "Well, in my world, a wedding means something. It's—it's *sacred*."

"Ivy, you're being childish," he started.

She wouldn't let him finish. "I'm being childish? You're the one who is falling for these stupid games." She jabbed a finger at his chest. "Don't you get it? Brunelli is testing you. He's testing *us*. He wants to see how far we'll go to get his signature. He doesn't want to see a loveless marriage any more than I do."

Daniel's face was somber and the look in his eyes unreadable. This was the man who had shown up at her door in Brooklyn, the man who had offered to pay for her silence. This was a stranger.

"I honestly don't care what his motives are. He's agreed that if this marriage occurs, he will sign the deal. No questions asked. The lawyers have already drawn up the paperwork. You can get an annulment immediately after the ceremony if you'd like."

"If I'd like," she repeated. "If *I'd* like. What about you, Daniel? What is it that you'd like? Do you really want to see me marry another man?"

He shrugged. "Honestly, Ivy, I don't care who you marry once this deal is done. But for now, yes, I would like very much to watch you walk down the aisle to marry Jack."

"I thought you...." She swallowed back tears and tried again. "I thought we had something. I thought you cared—"

His sigh of exasperation cut off her trail of words. "Listen, Ivy, I'm sorry if you got the wrong impression. It was stupid of me to sleep with you. I should have known you couldn't handle it." He made a face of disgust. "You still believe in fairy tales."

Ivy gaped at him in horror. Who was this man? She tried to speak but couldn't get past the lump in her throat. This Daniel was a stranger to her—a cruel, cold-hearted stranger.

"But I made it clear from the very beginning—nothing is going to get in the way of this merger going through. Certainly not some silly fling."

She flinched. There was that word again. She couldn't speak. If she opened her mouth she wouldn't be able to keep the tears at bay. But he wasn't done. "We had a deal, remember? You signed up to do everything that was required of you to make the merger a reality. If you bail on me now, our contract is null and void. There will be no money, no promotion—hell, you'll be lucky if you have your old job waiting for you."

She tried to will away the tears that were threatening to spill in the face of Daniel's cold glare. Please stop talking. One more hurtful word from this man—the man she loved—it would be her undoing.

"You don't mean that," she said. He turned away from her but she moved to block his path. The anger she'd felt this afternoon was returning in full force. "I don't know what's happened to you. I don't know why you're acting like this. But I know this isn't the real you. The Daniel I know would never be so cruel."

"Do you really think you know me so well?" he mocked.

"Yes," she shot back. "Or at least I thought I did." She swallowed a lump in her throat. Maybe she was the one who had been wrong all along. Maybe *this* was the real Daniel and the man she'd had an affair with was a façade. He could have been using her all along. Hadn't he told her from the beginning that he would do whatever it took to make this deal happen? What if that included seducing the infatuated idiot from Ohio?

"Did you..." her voice trailed off. She cleared her throat to try again. "Did you sleep with me to get me to play along with this charade?"

His silence was deafening. She searched his eyes for an emotion. Any emotion. But all she saw was the cold, hard glint of steel.

"Say something," she whispered.

His answer was a shrug. "What do you want me to say? I told you from the very beginning that this was always about business."

She struggled for a response. "I thought you cared about me." She hated how weak her voice sounded compared to his matter-of-fact tone.

"You're a little girl, Ivy. A little girl in love."

Ivy opened her mouth to protest but she couldn't. A little sob escaped her lips when she tried to speak. It was the truth. But the way he said it—it was an accusation. It was a damning judgment.

He laughed off her unspoken protest. "Oh, please. It's written all over your face."

Disbelief warred with anger. He was laughing at her. He had dealt a deathblow to her heart and now he was laughing at her?

"How can you do this to me?" The words were torn from her. Even she could hear the desperate sadness that laced her voice. Her heart was exposed and vulnerable…and this man could not care less.

He reached out a hand and brushed a curl back from her face in a pale imitation of tenderness. "I told you, Ivy. Everyone has a choice and you made yours. No one is forcing you to do anything."

That touch was her undoing. The tears that had been threatening to spill finally fell and trickled down her cheeks. Still, he remained unfazed.

"You're right, I did make my choice," she said, forcing the words out despite the tremble in her voice. "I chose to go along with this farce for my parents' sake and my own." She swallowed the thick lump in her throat, all hope of maintaining pride long since gone. "I…I also chose you. I chose to give myself to you and to trust you. I—I chose to love you."

The only reaction she got was a tick in his jaw and a weary exhale.

"I made my choice and now it seems you have made yours," she continued. "You chose money over love and now you have to live with it."

His lips curved into a scornful smile at that and the look he gave her could only be described as pitying. "Ivy. Don't you get it? There was never a debate, no choice to be made. For men like me, it always comes down to business. Loving you was never even an option."

The tears came harder and faster as the words struck their target. She felt like she'd been punched in the gut as all of the air rushed out of her lungs.

"Get out." The words came out quietly as she choked for air. She took a deep breath and said it louder. "Get out!"

* * * *

Ivy couldn't sleep. She wanted to call her parents or Holly but she couldn't bear to tell them everything—not now at least. But she needed help; she needed advice.

Throwing off the covers, she padded through the villa's cool, tiled hallway toward the kitchen. Maybe a little warm milk would help her to relax and get some sleep.

The light was already on in the kitchen and she found Brunelli, clad in a bulky robe, eating leftovers from dinner. He beckoned her to come in with a guilty smile. "You caught me," he said in a hushed voice. He held out a fork and offered up the leftovers. She shook her head. "I was looking for something to drink."

"Trouble sleeping?"

She nodded and poured herself a glass of milk as he chewed his food. "This is my fault, I'm afraid," he said.

She tried to muster a smile. She couldn't argue that. His ridiculous wedding plan had ruined everything. No, that wasn't altogether fair. She had gotten herself into this web of lies and it was Daniel who had broken her heart.

She chose her words carefully. "I want to make everyone happy. But, at what cost?"

He nodded and not for the first time she wondered how much he truly knew about her situation. "You don't want the wedding here?"

Ivy sighed. "This might be the most amazing wedding venue I've ever seen." She had a flickering image of walking through the veranda on her father's arm, Daniel's warm gaze watching her walk toward him. She mentally trashed that daydream. *Let it go, Ivy. He's not the man you fell in love with. You fell in love with an impostor.*

"I would love to have my wedding here," she said truthfully. "Someday."

"Ah," he nodded in understanding. "There is no rush, my dear. You and Jack are welcome to have the wedding here anytime."

She shot him a look of surprise. "And the merger?"

He chuckled. "I'm afraid I cannot budge there. The merger must wait until the wedding is over. I need to be sure of the people I'm dealing with."

Ivy watched this kind old man eat his leftovers and wanted to scream in frustration. *Why are you doing this to me?*

He studied his food as though some answer could be found in the cold pasta. "You love Jack, yes?"

"Yes." *As a friend*, she added in her head. "And I know this merger means the world to him. So, on one hand, I want to get married and make everyone happy."

He glanced up in surprise at the "everyone" part. But how could she explain how much this deal would mean to not just Jack but her family as well. *And Daniel*, a traitorous voice said.

"But it's not what you want," he finished for her.

She shook her head. "Not like this. When I marry, I want it to be on my terms, not for ulterior motives."

He nodded in sympathy, seemingly oblivious to the fact that with one word he could end this dilemma. He could solve everyone's problems.

They sat in silence for a bit, lost in thought. When she'd finished her milk and stood to leave, he stopped her. "What will you do, my dear?"

She smiled in resignation. "There's really no question. I'll do whatever it takes to make the people I love happy."

He walked over and gave her a kiss on the cheek. "Well then, let me be the first to kiss the bride."

* * * *

Daniel thought he might drown in self-hatred. He couldn't bear to look at himself in the mirror as he poured another shot of whiskey into an empty glass. *I did it for her*, he told himself for the millionth time. *It was for her own good.*

But it was no use. Not even that rationalization could assuage the gut-wrenching guilt he felt every time he envisioned Ivy's face when he'd mocked her love or the sound of her shaky voice when she tried to reason with him.

He was a devil—worse than his father. All the more reason she was better off without him. But he couldn't help but wonder if he were better off without her.

Daniel gulped down the burning liquid to quiet that nagging voice that was screaming at him to chase after her. It was begging him to make things right. Tell her he hadn't meant any of it. He loved her. He loved her more than he'd ever known possible. And yet he'd hurt her.

Daniel smashed his glass against the wall at the memory of Ivy's beautiful eyes filled with tears as he'd cruelly and matter-of-factly denied his feeling for her. He was the cause of all that pain so clearly written on her face and in her eyes. He'd broken her heart.

His own heart felt as smashed and battered as the glass that lay in pieces at his feet. He had broken both of their hearts. And what for? He could barely remember. The whiskey was doing too good of a job blurring his memory.

He sank into an armchair and dropped his head into his hands. He forced himself to relive his childhood. Replay the hurt and loneliness his mother experienced every day of his young life.

That was why. He had to remember that. He had to hang onto that memory for dear life. She might be hurting today but she would be better off in the end.

And you? That traitorous voice asked. *Will you be better off?*

That was the whiskey talking. It was bringing out every selfish desire in his body. It was begging him to go to her now and take her into his arms and never let go.

He could drop down on his knees and beg her forgiveness and make it all go away. He could tell Brunelli to take his deal and shove it and live happily ever after with the woman that he loved. But he wouldn't. He'd chosen his path years ago and there was no turning back. He heaved himself out of the chair and turned on the shower.

A shower would sober him and remind him of his choices.

Ivy had been right about that. He had made the decision to choose the merger over her, just like he'd made the choice to walk away from his family all those years ago. It was for the best then and it was in Ivy's best interests now.

With sobriety would come the strength of will to see this farce through, for Ivy's sake if for nothing else. She deserved better and he would see that she got it.

* * * *

Ivy had made her decision and there was no turning back. She told Brunelli that despite her protests earlier, she did not want her friends and family flown out for the ceremony. There was no way she would ever be able to go through with such a farce if they were there. He seemed to understand and shooed her off to her room, telling her to get some rest. He and his family would handle all of the details.

She padded back to her room, but paused halfway there. There was one thing she needed to do before she would ever be able to sleep.

She tapped softly on Daniel's door. She knew he would be awake but she was careful not to rouse anyone else in the household. He answered the door clad only in a pair of sweatpants. The muscles in his chest were defined by the soft glow of the bedside lamp and his face was cast in shadows.

"What are you doing here?"

Not exactly a warm welcome, but then what had she expected? A glimmer of the man she'd thought she'd known perhaps? She had to scoff at her own naiveté. It was becoming extremely apparent that man never existed. She had been fooled by a world-class con man.

"May I come in?" When he hesitated, she rolled her eyes. "Don't worry, I'm not here to cause a scene, but there a few things we need to discuss. I'd rather not wake the others."

He opened the door wider and she slid past him. She tried to ignore his heady scent and his warmth. He must have just showered because his hair was damp and it fell into his eyes giving him a roguish look.

She turned to face him and steeled herself for what she was about to say. She knew it was over between them; he'd made that abundantly clear. And she knew what she had to do for Jack and for her parents, but she had to spell it out for him. Humiliating as it might be, she knew that if she didn't give him every opportunity to make things right, she would always wonder. He may be able to throw away everything they had without a second thought but it was not in her to be so blasé about love. And that's what it was. Or at least, that's what she'd thought they'd had.

"I came here to tell you that I'll do it. I'll marry Jack in two days so you can have your precious merger."

She thought she saw his jaw twitch but couldn't be sure in the dim light. His eyes were cast in shadows and his expression gave nothing away.

"Thank you."

Her laugh was humorless. "Don't thank me, I'm not doing this for you. I'm doing this for Jack and my parents."

"I understand. You've made the right choice."

She searched his face for any sign of the man she loved. "There's one more thing."

He waited in silence for her to continue.

"After all of this is over, I never want to see you again. Is that clear? By trying to force me to do this—ordering me to marry another man—you're throwing everything away between us."

He rubbed a hand over his face and sighed. She supposed he thought she was being childish again. And maybe she was. Maybe she was a hopeless romantic who believed in knights in shining armor and happy ever afters. But that didn't mean she was wrong.

"Before you tell me again that this was just some *fling*," she spit the word out in disgust. "Let me tell you this. You're wrong. You. Are.

Wrong." She enunciated each word and watched as his jaw clenched at her tone. So he didn't like being treated like a child either? Tough.

She crossed her arms and said a little prayer that she could say what she needed to say without bursting into tears. "I don't know if you're lying to yourself as well as me but I know what love is when I experience it. I know that what we had was more than a fling—it meant something."

He still didn't speak and she let out a sad laugh.

"Well, it meant something to me at any rate. But the moment I walk out this door, we're through. Your decision has been made; you chose this merger over me. And let me tell you something—you made the wrong choice."

Ivy walked past him to the door and walked through it, never looking back. She'd said what she'd come to say.

* * * *

Daniel couldn't concentrate to save his life.

"I got another pawn," his grandfather crowed. Daniel grimaced. It was humiliating how efficiently his grandfather was kicking his butt at chess. The old man pocketed his white pawn and beckoned to one of his granddaughters to refill his water glass.

Daniel couldn't get over how old he looked. The last decade had taken its toll, and it was difficult to unite the tough, weathered man who'd helped raise him with the frail man who sat across from him. There was no doubt that Brunelli had been telling the truth when he said his grandfather was running out of time. He needed to thank him for making sure they reconciled while they still had a chance. He owed Brunelli a debt of gratitude—and Ivy, too.

He saw her clear as day in his mind's eye. Standing in his room, the warm lamplight turning her hair into a fiery halo around her head. That's what Ivy was, he thought, a fiery, passionate angel. And she could have been his.

"What's wrong with you, Danny? You look like something the cat dragged home. Did you sleep at all last night?" His grandfather might look frail but he still had the same gruff way of talking.

"No, Grandpa, I didn't get much sleep." He took his turn, not bothering to strategize. This game was as good as over. He didn't feel the need to expound on why he hadn't slept. How could he explain that he'd been haunted by images of what could have been? He needed to pull it together. He'd made his decision and he had to see it through. Besides, he told himself for the millionth time—it was for her own good.

She'll have it annulled, he reminded himself. But he knew very well that wasn't the point. Ivy had been raised to respect vows and traditions. She put family first. She valued love above all.

She loved him. No, she *thought* she loved him. There's a difference. They hadn't been together long—she would move on in no time. That thought brought an excruciating jolt of jealousy. He hated the thought of her with another man.

"Earth to Daniel, yoo-hoo."

Daniel smiled. "Sorry, Grandpa."

"If I wanted to play chess against a zombie I would have taken the set down to the morgue."

"Very funny." Daniel moved his rook and ordered himself to concentrate.

His grandfather was watching him and when he spoke, he was unusually serious. "I'm glad you came to see me, Danny. It means a lot to an old man."

"It means a lot to me too, Grandpa. I'm sorry it took me so long to get here."

His grandfather's smile was a mirror image of his own. "You're stubborn just like me. Just like your mother."

Daniel looked down and pretended to study the board. He couldn't stand to see the pride in his grandfather's eyes. He was nothing like him and definitely nothing like his mother. He was his father's son through and through.

"So tell me, Danny boy, how is a man like you not married? You've got good looks and the Italian charm. What, you haven't met the right woman yet?"

Daniel saw auburn hair and a pixie face. He shook his head. "Marriage and family aren't in the cards for me."

"Why not?" He looked up to see his grandfather frowning at him.

"Because I have different priorities. I decided to follow in my father's footsteps, for better or worse. And you and I both know there is no room in that world for a career and a family. I won't make the same mistake as him and try to have my cake and eat it too." He gave his grandfather a knowing look. "The people you care about end up getting hurt."

His grandfather nodded. "I see, so you've decided to eliminate the risk by doing away with family altogether."

Daniel looked up to see his grandfather laughing at him. "My boy, that is the stupidest logic I have ever heard."

He didn't think he'd ever seen his grandfather laugh so hard. "Excuse me?"

"Oh, you heard me. I'm glad your mother can't hear you talking like that."

Daniel sputtered a bit. His grandfather had always been the one person who could render him speechless.

"You were there, Grandpa, you know how much pain my father caused everyone. Like it or not, I'm his son. I made the choice to follow in his footsteps and I've never regretted that decision."

"Your father wasn't a bad man, Daniel, he just made bad choices." Daniel was surprised by the intensity in the old man's eyes. "Your father recognized his mistake when your mother died. He realized that he'd gotten his priorities all screwed up. And I think he tried to make up for that with you. Why do you think he was so insistent on you coming to work for him?"

Daniel couldn't answer and his grandfather didn't give him a chance. "I'll tell you why. He wanted to spend time with you before it was too late. He wanted to make up for all the time he'd missed when you were young."

His grandfather shook his head and Daniel tried not to squirm like a little kid in the face of the old man's disappointment. "It was bad enough that your father made the poor choices that he did. But to see you making the exact same mistakes..." his voice trailed off and he looked every bit his age as he leaned back in his chair with an exhausted sigh.

His grandfather tried to lighten the mood a bit. "Or maybe you've never fallen in love. Is that it? Maybe you haven't found the one."

Something in Daniel's expression must have given him away because the old man's eyes softened. "Don't be a fool, Danny."

"I don't want to hurt her." The words came out strangled. His voice could barely be heard over the sound of children playing. But his grandfather heard him and he leaned across the table to squeeze his hand.

"The only way you can hurt the ones you love is to push them away. Take my word for it." The old man's eyes glistened with unshed tears. "Now go to her, Danny. Don't wait until it's too late."

* * * *

Ivy and Jack found themselves in wedding planning central that morning. It turned out Brunelli and his family were amazingly efficient party planners and the happy couple's sole job seemed to be giving the final nod of approval once everything had been selected, from the flowers to the music.

Ivy felt like she was in some sort of bizarre dream world as her life was planned right in front of her eyes. She sat there with a slightly dazed expression and tried not to think too hard about what it was they were planning.

This will all be over soon. You'll be back in your studio apartment with your job at the hotel and everyone will have forgotten about Jack Everett's failed marriage. She'd tell her family everything and they would forgive her in time. And they would be taken care of financially, that was the important thing.

The internal pep talk did the trick. It kept her placid and quiet as she accepted the fact that her wedding—the event she'd dreamed of since she was a little girl—was going to be the most miserable lie of her life.

She wasn't sure what was going through Jack's mind during the planning session; he was abnormally quiet as well. When he finally spoke up, everyone looked surprised.

"Could we have a moment please?"

The Brunelli clan stared at him with wide eyes. "I'd like a moment alone with my fiancée, if you don't mind."

Brunelli himself ushered the group out of the room, telling them to take their time. "What is it?" she asked him once they were alone.

He turned to her with the most serious expression she'd ever seen from him. "Ivy, you don't have to do this."

"What? What do you mean?"

Jack sighed and flopped back in his seat. "I mean, I hate to see you like this. You've already gone above and beyond for me and this merger but I can't ask you to go through with a fake wedding when you're so clearly in love with someone else."

Ivy was humiliated to find tears filling her eyes. She'd gone all morning without a single tear but at the mere mention of love, she went to pieces. Jack's eyes widened with concern.

"Ivy, what is it?"

She sniffled a bit before the words came out in a watery voice. "He doesn't want me."

Jack's expression went from shocked to confused to royally enraged in a heartbeat. She didn't think she'd ever seen Jack angry and the sight was rather shocking. "Of course he does. The man is head over heels for you. If he says otherwise, he's lying."

Ivy gave him a weak smile. "Even if he does, he won't admit it. He made his decision and I've made mine." She explained to him about her family's finances and her job. He shrugged. "I've still got some money left. I'll help you and your family out—it's the least I can do to repay you for these last couple of weeks."

Ivy's mouth opened and closed a couple of times as she digested his offer. "But what about the merger? Jack, this means everything to you. You've been working so hard for this."

He sat back and shot her a rueful smile. "I'll admit, I'm bummed that I won't get to see this particular dream come true, but I'll find another way. Brunelli isn't the only manufacturing tycoon out there. And there have got to be other investors who'll take a chance on me if Daniel decides he's out."

"You would do that for me?" The tears were outright spilling down her cheeks now and he pulled her in for a hug.

"Your happiness is more important than a merger."

Ivy let out a hiccup sob against his chest. What she wouldn't give to hear Daniel say those words.

They were both startled by the sound of someone clapping in the doorway.

"Bravo, Jack. Bravo." They looked up in surprise to see Brunelli beaming at them in the doorway. At their shocked looks, he added, "*Mi scusi*, but the acoustics in this place…." He waved his arms as he struggled to find the words. "No secret is safe in the villa."

He'd heard everything. Ivy sat up and shot Jack a quick look but he seemed resigned to the fact that the deal was over. He gave her a little shrug along with his devil-may-care grin.

"Well, I guess that cat is out of the bag," Jack said under his breath.

The waited for Brunelli to say something, to call them out on the lies or lecture them on trying to fool him but he was still standing there in the doorway, smiling for all the world like he'd just gotten married himself.

Maybe he hadn't heard everything or, maybe he thought that Jack was offering to postpone their wedding for her sake.

It was time to come clean. She shared a look with Jack and at his nod of approval, she started, "Brunelli, we need to explain—"

He cut her off by leaning toward the doorway and bellowing out in Italian. Angelo came running with a piece of paper and a pen.

"What are you doing?" Ivy asked.

"I'm signing the merger contract."

Jack and Ivy looked from one another to Brunelli and back again. "You're signing it? But why?" Jack asked. "The wedding is off."

"*Si*, the wedding is off, that is what is so fantastic." He caught their look of confusion and laughed in their faces. "It's so simple, *bella donna*. You love Daniel and Daniel loves you—"

"So you know?" Jack interrupted. "How long have you known?"

Brunelli gave him a look that said he clearly doubted the younger man's sanity. "Please, my friend, give me some credit."

"But Jack and I…we've been lying to you," Ivy said. She had to be sure he understood. Her mind was scrambling to make sense of the sudden turn of events.

"I know, I know it all and I couldn't be more pleased that you finally put an end to this silly show." Brunelli turned to Jack. "What you just did—what you said to Ivy, that proves that you are the man I want to work with." He turned to Ivy with a knowing look and patted his heart. "He has soul."

Ivy laughed and accepted the handkerchief he handed her. "He definitely does."

After that, things moved quickly. As fast as the wedding was planned, it was dismantled. The Brunelli's were a well-oiled machine of industry.

Ivy went back to her room to pack up her belongings and figure out what to do next. She couldn't go back to the hotel. Not yet, at least. There, Daniel would be her boss. Even if she didn't see him on a day-to-day basis, she would be looking for him, straining to catch sight of him or hear his name mentioned.

No. She needed a clean break. Someplace where she could heal her broken heart and start again. She needed to go home.

There was a knock on her door and for one fleeting moment, there was a flicker of hope inside of her that Daniel would be on the other side. She tried not to let her disappointment show when she saw Lucia standing there, wearing a sad, sympathetic smile.

Would she ever stop holding out hope? She hoped so. It was hope that caused her heart to break over and over again.

She forced a smile she didn't feel as she motioned to Lucia to come in. She went back to folding and packing, unable to summon up the energy to be polite. For a little while she thought Lucia may not speak at all, she hovered in the doorway, watching Ivy's progress.

"I'm sorry to see you go," she said. "I'm sorry you're leaving like this"

Ivy glanced up with a wry smile. "I suppose you heard the truth from your grandfather?"

Lucia's grin was mischievous. "I didn't need Grandpa to tell me what's underneath my nose."

Ivy dropped the pair of pants she'd been folding and turned to gape. "You knew?" At Lucia's broad smile she let out a sigh of exasperation. "Did everyone know? Was everyone just laughing at us behind our backs all week?"

Lucia looked horrified. "No, of course not! Grandpa and I are the only ones who knew. And it was you who told me."

Ivy stared at the young woman. "What are you talking about?"

Lucia wagged a finger teasingly. "I had my suspicions from the very beginning. The way you and Daniel looked at one another…" her voice trailed off with a romantic sigh that made Ivy want to vomit. She didn't doubt Lucia had seen love in her eyes, but Daniel?

"And then when the two of you disappeared at the festival?" she added with a knowing look that made Ivy blush, despite herself.

"That's when I decided to test my theory. "Lucia was looking at her with an expectant look. When Ivy just turned back to her luggage, Lucia sighed. "I was testing you," she said, placing herself in front of Ivy. "The other night at dinner…" Lucia let out a high-pitched girly giggle and gave Ivy a flirtatious look. The same look she'd been throwing Daniel's way at dinner the other night. The night she had been ready to—

"I thought you were going to claw my eyes out," Lucia said with a laugh.

Ivy just stared at the other woman for several seconds before laughing herself. The laughter felt incongruous after so many tears.

Maybe there was hope for her yet.

Lucia held up her left hand, where a diamond ring that Ivy hadn't noticed glittered in the dim light. "Maybe I forgot to mention that I am happily engaged." She gave a little shrug. "How do you say…'my bad'?" she said with a mischievous grin.

When Lucia reached out to give her a hug, Ivy stepped into her embrace and as quickly as she'd started to laugh, she was choking back tears.

"I'm sorry," she said in a choked voice. "I seem to be a bit of a mess."

Lucia just held her tighter. "Don't give up on him, *mia amica*. I may not know much about the world but I know love and that man is head over heels."

Ivy nodded as she pulled back from the embrace. How could she explain that whether Daniel loved her or not, it didn't matter if he didn't choose to follow his heart?

Lucia was almost at the door when she stopped and turned back. "I almost forgot, I wanted you to have this." She held out a drawing. Ivy's breath caught in her throat at the sketch. It was clearly Ivy and she was wearing the most beautiful dress Ivy had ever seen.

"Your wedding dress," Lucia explained. "I thought I would try out my designs...."

"It's gorgeous," Ivy said with a sigh. She went to hand the sketch back but Lucia shook her head. "You keep it. You may still need it."

She opened her mouth to protest but Lucia had already slipped out.

Ivy didn't see Daniel for the rest of the day. The Brunelli clan fell over themselves to help her—from booking her plane ticket home to arranging for a ride to the airport. She'd insisted on leaving on the next flight home and Angelo was recruited to be her driver.

Jack offered to come along with her to the airport but she refused. He seemed to understand that she was through talking for the moment. She was done with being comforted and consoled by her well-intentioned new friends.

Ivy needed to be alone with her thoughts and, most importantly, far, far away from Daniel and all of the people and places she associated with him. Jack helped her with her bags as she and Angelo loaded up the car but she kept their goodbye short and simple.

"I'll see you when I get back to New York," she said.

He gave her a quick hug and whispered in her ear, "he's an idiot."

* * * *

Don't wait until it's too late. Daniel's grandfather's words echoed in his skull as he sped through the winding, country roads that led back to the Brunelli's villa. He couldn't let her go through with this. How had he ever thought he could?

His grandfather was right; he was making the same mistakes as his father. He was choosing business and money over love and family. The older man had gone on to tell him the stories from his perspective, which was so very different from his own. As a child all he'd seen was how hurt his mother had been. How hurt *he* had been. He hadn't seen the love they'd shared when they first married or watched the trail of bad choices that his father had made which led him so far astray.

Daniel sucked in the fresh air of the land he loved so much. He still had a chance to make this right. He wasn't destined to make the same choices as his father. He could get it right. He could make her happy. He could give her the kind of love and commitment she deserved.

Maggie Dallen

I'm not going to throw it all away over some fling. His words came back to haunt him and he pounded on the steering wheel, furious with himself for being so blind.

But she loved him. She told him so in his room the night before. He could salvage this, he knew he could. He would tell Brunelli everything and cancel this sham of a wedding. He would drop down on his knees and beg, if that's what it took to get her forgiveness.

The villa was unusually quiet when he entered. He couldn't even hear the usual patter of children's feet that seemed to constantly fill the home. He went from room to room looking for Ivy—looking for *anyone*.

When finally he reached the back veranda, he found Brunelli and Jack sipping on wine, deep in conversation. They both looked up in mild surprise when he burst in on them.

"I'm calling off the wedding."

The two men looked at one another and burst out laughing. Daniel fumed. He had just put an end to the deal they'd been negotiating for weeks and they were laughing? "Did you hear me? The wedding is off. If that means you want to take your business elsewhere, than that's what you'll have to do."

Brunelli threw his hands up in mock surrender while Jack struggled to stop laughing.

"The wedding is already off, Danny, you can stop yelling."

"And the merger has been signed. Come, join us for a celebratory drink," Brunelli said.

Daniel gaped at them, his brain trying to keep up with the sudden turn of events. "But where—how?"

Jack patted the seat beside him while Brunelli poured another glass. "Have a seat, old man, and we'll tell you everything."

He shook his head. First thing's first. "Where's Ivy? I need to talk to her."

At that, Jack and Brunelli stopped laughing. Jack gave his friend a look of pity. "She's gone, buddy. I'm sorry."

"What do you mean she's gone?"

"I mean, she's flying over the Atlantic as we speak. Once we canceled the wedding, she decided she didn't want to stick around. I think she needed to be with family for a while. She booked the next flight out of here."

There was a heavy silence as both men glared up at Daniel in undisguised judgment. Goddammit. They knew about him and Ivy.

He dropped down into the seat beside Jack and dropped his head into his hands. "Is she all right?" his voice came out muffled from behind his hands.

"She is young and she is strong," Brunelli said. "She will recover."

Daniel felt a stab of pain. He had hurt her. He had done what he'd sworn not to do—he'd hurt the one he loved. He was an idiot.

"I'm an idiot." There was a silence that screamed of agreement amongst the other two men.

Brunelli allowed Daniel approximately one minute to wallow in his guilt and then he banged on the table with a makeshift gavel. "All right, gentleman, time to get down to business. How is Daniel going to win her back?"

Daniel sat up straight, with new purpose. If there was one thing he was good at it was coming up with a plan. He had ruined the best thing that ever happened to him with a plan, he could sure as hell fix it with one, too.

And so the three men, newly minted partners, spent the rest of the evening plotting and planning to pull off the comeback of the century.

Chapter 9

The flight home felt like an eternity. Trapped in a public setting with nothing to do but obsess over every ugly word or every tender kiss, it was a miracle she arrived in Ohio with her sanity intact.

Ivy showed up on her parents' doorstep with tears streaming down her cheeks and a suitcase in her hand. Despite the fact that she was jet lagged and travel weary, she told them everything the moment she arrived. They were angry, as she'd expected. But it was the hurt in their eyes when they realized the depth of the lies she'd told that made her heart ache. She never wanted to see that look again. She'd destroyed their trust and now it was up to her to rebuild it.

Her parents had put all that aside out of concern. They knew their daughter well—she didn't have to tell them that she was heartbroken, it was written all over her face. Her mother had made her a cup of tea as she sobbed her way through the whole messy story.

The next morning, Ivy burrowed under the quilt that her grandmother made in the bed where she'd slept for most of her life. She could hear her parents bustling about in the kitchen, making coffee, and getting breakfast started. She should go down and help, but the coward that she was, she didn't want to go down and face them.

There was a knock on her bedroom door. "Ivy? Are you awake?"

"Go away, Holly."

The door opened a crack as Holly ignored her. She poked her head into the room. "I come bearing tea and chocolate."

Ivy threw down the covers so she could see her sister. She was in fact, holding a tray filled with teacups and what looked to be chocolate muffins. She scowled. "Fine, but I don't want to talk, I just want the chocolate."

"Fair enough."

Ivy nibbled at the muffin but her stomach churned in protest. If she couldn't even muster up a proper appetite for chocolate, the situation was dire indeed.

"I suppose Mom and Dad filled you in?"

"To the fact that you're a big fat liar? Yeah, they filled me in."

Ivy breathed a sigh of relief. If her sister could joke about it, then they would be okay.

Holly pointed an accusatory finger in her face. "Oh no you don't. Don't go thinking you're off the hook just because you're all pitiful and sad. Once you cheer up a bit, you're going to have a lot of groveling to do."

"Understood."

"Okay then." Holly watched her picking at the muffin and sighed. "You really are pitiful, do you know that?"

Ivy's lower lip jutted out as she fought back a heaving sob. "I know."

Holly joined her on the bed and wrapped her arms around her like she used to do doing thunderstorms. "I really am sorry that I lied to you, Holly," Ivy said between hiccupping sobs.

Holly patted her back. "I know, sis. You can start to make it up to me by telling me everything—I mean the unedited story. I want to hear all the stuff you left out in the parental version."

And so Ivy let it all out, starting from the very beginning when Jack had chosen to hide from an angry husband behind her hostess stand and ending with Angelo dropping her off at the airport.

"I'm pretty sure I scared the kid off of women for life," Ivy said while wiping her nose. "Poor Angelo looked like a deer in headlights when I started sobbing in the car."

"Oh, honey." Holly pulled her in for a hug and rested her chin on Ivy's head. "Sounds like you fell hard for this guy."

"I thought—I thought I *loved* him." She pushed herself away so she could look at her sister. "I thought I knew him. I thought he felt the same way. I thought—I thought..." She trailed off and fell back against the pillows. "Oh, how could I have gotten it so wrong? I feel like an idiot."

"You are not the idiot. He is. Or else he's a damn good actor."

Ivy shrugged. She didn't know what to believe anymore.

Holly persisted, "You've always been a good judge of character. And you're the last person in the world who would fall for some guy just because you've got the hots for him."

Ivy sniffed. "I guess."

"Well, I know it for a fact." She faced Ivy with folded arms and a grim stare. "I am giving you approximately five more minutes to wallow in your little pity party and then I am dragging you out of bed and into the sunshine. Got it?"

Ivy knew better than to argue with her sister when she got that look. She nodded meekly. "Got it."

Ten minutes later, Ivy dug out weeds in her parents' garden. It was one of many chores her mother had lined up as punishment for the lies.

It actually felt good to be doing manual labor. Getting her hands dirty and working up a sweat at least managed to distract her from memories of Daniel and the decisions she couldn't avoid much longer. Sooner or later she would have to decide what to do next. She couldn't live with her parents forever but the thought of returning to New York was more than she could handle. She focused on the dirt and weeds in front of her and for a brief moment, everything else fell to the wayside.

Her time in Italy almost seemed like a bad dream when her hands were firmly planted in her family's land. She tried not to dwell on the fact that the land would almost certainly have to be sold off now that she'd failed her parents—now that she'd failed *everyone*. Her parents were too proud to accept charity from Jack, even if he was nice enough to offer. And if she couldn't go back to her old job, she would have to move back in with them and be an even bigger burden. Good Lord, she'd made a mess of every area of her life. *That's what happens when you make a deal with the devil.*

Ivy jabbed at the dirt with a spade. At this rate she would probably kill as many flowers as weeds. More guilt gnawed at her as she now ruined her mother's garden as well as her life. She sat back and wiped a hand across her sweaty brow.

What she needed was a plan. A strategy. That was what Daniel would do, wasn't it? It's probably what he's doing right now, she thought. Her lips compressed and her eyes narrowed into a glare as she clawed at the earth with her bare hands. Daniel and his strategies, she fumed. She could just see him plotting away in his room at the villa. He was his generation's Machiavelli.

But no, he had gotten what he'd wanted, she reminded herself. The merger was signed—no thanks to her. So everyone got what they wanted—Daniel, Jack, Brunelli—she was the only one who had walked away empty-handed. So maybe Daniel wasn't the idiot here. Maybe *she* was the one who needed to have her brain checked.

"Ivy!" Her mom was calling from the back porch. When Ivy glanced up her mother waved the house phone above her head. "Phone for you, dear."

Daniel. Her heart leapt in her chest. She took a deep breath and reminded herself that she was making an attempt to be a little brighter these days. Of course it wasn't Daniel. Why on earth would he call her? He'd gotten what he'd wanted and now she was neatly out of his life, without a payout and without a job. He could move on to his next victim scot-free.

Ivy made her way to the house slowly. Her heart was still racing. Despite all the logic that her brain was spewing there was a little part of her—okay, a big part of her—that was praying fervently that it was Daniel on the line. Ivy groaned aloud. She really *was* an idiot. And a glutton for punishment to boot. Her mother gave her an encouraging smile when she handed her the phone.

"Hello?"

"Ivy, thank God. I've been trying to track you down all morning."

"Hey Jack."

"Why isn't your cell on?"

She shrugged, momentarily forgetting he couldn't see her. "I don't know. I guess the battery died." Some distant part of her brain was aware that her voice was unusually lethargic and was trying to snap her out of whatever depressed funk she'd slipped into but her heart and body were not up to the challenge. She let herself slide down against the kitchen wall and cradled the phone against her cheek.

"What do you want, Jack?"

"How are you holding up?"

"I'm okay."

"You're a lousy liar."

"Well, I guess that's why Brunelli never bought us as a couple, huh?"

"Nah, it wasn't our acting that gave us away. It was you and Danny."

Ivy's chin snapped up at the mention of his name. There was a short silence as Ivy debated whether or not she should ask about him. No. She didn't want to hear about him. She'd clearly developed some sort of strange obsession with the man. Cold turkey was best.

"So what's up, Jack?"

"I wanted to let you know..." Jack trailed off and cleared his throat. Ivy was intrigued; she didn't think she'd ever heard Jack at a loss for words.

"What is it?"

"I want you to know that you'll always have a job with EverTech. Brunelli and I—we talked it over and you've been so valuable, such a team player. I just wanted you to know that."

Ivy swallowed a thick lump at the unexpected kindness. "Thanks Jack, I appreciate it, I really do."

"But?"

"But I can't go to work for Daniel. I just can't."

"Ivy, he won't be part of the day-to-day operations. He's already moving on to his next investment—"

"Please, Jack...."

There was a heavy silence. "Yeah, okay. I get it."

Ivy studied the dirt beneath her fingernails as she pondered what to say to this man who had become such a great friend in such a short period of time.

"Listen, Ivy, Brunelli and I want you to have the money you were promised." She tried to cut him off but he barreled ahead. "You earned every penny. Without you, this deal would never have happened. Besides, it's not for you, right? It's for your family. Don't make your family pay—"

"For my mistakes?" she finished. She knew he had a point but pride warred with practicality.

"I didn't say that."

She heaved a sigh. "I'll think about it, okay?"

"I guess that's all I can ask for. And Ivy, about Daniel...maybe you should—"

She cut him off, her heart hammering at the mention of his name. "I don't want to talk about him, Jack. I mean it."

She heard a familiar voice in the background and Jack stifled a laugh.

"Was that Brunelli?" she asked. "What did he say?"

"He said you're welcome to use his villa for your wedding whenever you want."

Ivy rolled her eyes. Those two certainly had a droll sense of humor. "Tell him thanks a lot. Maybe I'll take him up on that in a decade or so."

* * * *

Daniel drove through the winding back roads of Ivy's hometown in a state of panic. For the first time in his life he hadn't been able to come up with a plan. He needed to win over the woman he'd pushed away—the love of his life—and he had no idea how he was going to go about it.

What he needed was a grand gesture—something to prove that he was the man for her. That he deserved her. But that was the problem. He didn't deserve her. They both knew it. He didn't deserve her trust or her love.

Muttering a curse under his breath, he contemplated turning the car around and heading back to the airport for the millionth time since he set out that morning. Glancing down at the address written on an envelope, he cursed again. He felt like he'd been driving around in circles for hours.

Maybe that was for the best. This was buying him some time to figure out what he would say. He had spent the past twenty-four hours doing nothing else with no success, but hell, maybe twenty more minutes of driving in circles would do the trick.

The Sinclair home was a modest ranch house with white clapboard siding, dark green shutters, and an immaculate lawn. He stared at it intently for about five minutes before he became aware of the attention he'd unintentionally brought to himself.

Daniel smiled at the young neighbor boy, who was gawking at him— or rather, at his Jaguar. He suspected sports cars were not the norm in this middle-class neighborhood.

He climbed out of the car and a voice stopped him. "Are you lost?" It was an older man with silver hair who was watering the hedge between the Sinclair house and what Daniel assumed was the man's home.

"No, sir, I don't believe I am. I'm looking for the Sinclairs." An elderly woman popped out of the neighbors' house and she ignored Daniel to address the man with the hose. "Who is it? Another one of those reporters?"

"I don't know, he didn't say." They were talking about him as if he wasn't there and Daniel was well aware of the young boy who was still staring at him, now with an open mouth.

A minivan slowed to a stop behind him. "Everything all right here, Mrs. Ferndale?"

Daniel tried not to let his exasperation show. "We're fine." He gave the man his best look of innocence, which only caused the bald, red-faced driver to squint at him with suspicion. "I was talking to Mrs. Ferndale."

"Right." He tried to maintain the polite smile but knew he was failing when all of the questioning faces around him turned to scowls. Daniel was half convinced he was about to be run out of town when he was saved by an older woman who cracked open the screen door of the Sinclair house. "What's going on out here?"

The woman was an older and taller version of Ivy with dark auburn curls that were pulled up into a ponytail. The woman held a broom in one hand and was shielding her eyes against the sun's glare with the other.

She pointed the broom handle at him in a not so welcoming manner. "Are you one of those damned reporters?"

Daniel shook his head. "Worse, I'm afraid. I'm that damned Daniel Gladwell."

By the look on her face, Daniel figured he had been right to assume that his name was the new curse word around the Sinclair house. "How do you do, ma'am?"

* * * *

"Ivy! Ivy, you'd better get in here."

She wiped away a bead of sweat that was trickling down the side of her nose.

"Ivy." It was her dad calling for her this time. He'd probably come up with another laundry list of chores for her to tackle. She had a feeling he was taking far too much pleasure in her punishment.

"I'm coming, I'm coming." She was still muttering to herself when she walked into the kitchen.

She froze in the doorway. *Daniel.* Like an oasis in the desert, he looked too good to be true standing in the kitchen of her parents' simple home. Ivy's heart threatened to leap out of her chest as her body began to tremble. Relief and joy rushed over her at the sight of him but they were quickly replaced with boiling hot rage.

"What are you doing here?" It came out so screechy that even her parents flinched at the sound.

Daniel looked quite calm. It was that cool exterior she knew so well. The sight of that perfectly poised charm made her that much angrier and she had visions of physical violence. That awful smile begged for a good punch.

"Don't smile at me like that," she said. She was horrified by how wobbly her voice sounded. That did the trick though. The smirk faded.

There was the real man. There was the man who had broken her heart.

Ivy didn't know whether she was going to scream or cry or leap into his arms. Before either of them found out, their little tableau was interrupted when Holly came barging into the kitchen, took in the scene before her and let out a little shriek of horror.

But it wasn't Daniel she was staring at, it was Ivy. She whirled around to face her parents. "Really? You are really going to let her stand there looking like that?"

Ivy looked around in confusion and that was when she caught sight of her reflection in the mirror above the kitchen table. She gasped aloud at the sight before her. There were streaks of mud and dirt all over her face and neck and her hair was a jumbled mess of curls atop her head with stray locks sticking out in every different direction.

Ivy saw Daniel's lips twitching as he struggled not to laugh. That was it. That was the last straw. She swatted her sister's hand out of her face before she could wipe her down with a washcloth.

Pointing a finger at Daniel, she glared at him with all of her might. "Don't you *dare*. Don't you dare laugh right now."

Daniel raised his hands in mock surrender. "I wouldn't dream of it."

She dropped her finger and took a step back. She refused to glance in the mirror lest she lose the anger that was holding her together.

"Ivy, please let me—"

"I don't want to hear it," she snapped. She clenched her hands into fists to stop their shaking.

He was silent for so long she didn't think he'd speak. All she could hear were his last words to her, the last conversation they had. "Why are you here, Daniel?" she repeated. "Do you need me to lie to the press for you? Come up with some excuse for why the wedding never happened?"

He flinched. "Ivy, I told you that we have choices—"

"And you made yours," she said. She hated how weak her voice sounded, how incredibly sad.

"I chose wrong," he said.

Ivy's chest tightened painfully. She heard Holly's intake of breath but other than that, their audience was watching in wide-eyed silence.

His eyes held hers for several long moments and in them she saw every emotion. For the first time since they'd met, he was completely unguarded. She saw fear, and heartbreak…and love.

Her breath caught in her throat as hope warred with fear. She could not take another blow to her heart.

"I asked you a question. What are you doing here?"

"I came here to ask your parents' permission."

Her eyes widened to the point where she felt them bugging out of her skull. "Permission for what?"

"To marry you."

Ivy stopped breathing. "What did you say?"

All eyes were on him but he only had eyes for her. She thought she might drown in the love she saw there—the pure, genuine, raw, unconditional love. Her heart ached with joy but she was struggling to hold on to her anger.

"You hurt me." The words came out haltingly, pulled from the depths of her pain.

He took a step closer and drew her into his arms. "Can you ever forgive me?"

She looked down at her hands that were trapped between them, keeping them apart. He used one finger to tip her chin so she was looking into his eyes and could see the honesty and emotions that no charming smile could hide.

"You told me once—you said, true love meant forgiveness and that everyone deserved a second chance."

She nodded a bit, tears threatening to spill. "Sometimes that's easier said than done."

He leaned down to drop a gentle kiss on the tip of her dirty nose. His words were so quiet she could feel her family moving in to try to hear him. "I solemnly vow that 'til my dying day, I will do everything in my power to make you happy."

"Why?" It came out as a whisper. She had to hear the words.

He pulled her closer and looked her straight in the eyes. "Because I love you, Ivy Sinclair. I love you more than life itself."

She heard her mother sigh and Holly start to whimper. Even her father sounded like he was sniffling, but Ivy was beaming. "I knew it! I knew you loved me. I knew I wasn't wrong about you."

Daniel laughed and she wrapped her arms around his neck. He planted a quick kiss on her lips. "And?" he prodded. "Now it's your turn."

She rolled her eyes with an exasperated sigh. "See how you're always ordering me around? When we get married, you've really got to work on that."

"Ivy," her name came out as a growl and he scooped her up into his arms so she was trapped against him. She wrapped her arms tightly around his neck. She never wanted to let go.

"I love you, too, Daniel."

She barely heard her family tiptoe out of the kitchen as Daniel's lips closed over hers and she found her new home.

Epilogue

Almost nine months later...

Ivy was curled up against Daniel on the veranda, tucked away in the corner for a moment of peace and quiet in the midst of all the revelry.

"Your grandfather looks happy."

"He is happy. His grandson has finally stopped acting like an idiot."

Ivy grinned. She never got tired of hearing him admit how wrong he'd been.

From where they were perched, they could see all of their family and friends laughing and dancing under the twinkling lights strung across the veranda. The hills of Tuscany were silhouetted against the twilight sky.

"Take a look at your parents," Daniel said. "Looks like they're fitting right in with the Italians. Who knew your mother could dance like that?"

"Who knew my husband could move like that?" Ivy teased.

He lightly kissed the top of her head "I can't believe the Brunellis made all of this happen so quickly."

Ivy nodded in agreement. The industrious Brunellis had come through with a last-minute wedding plan that would have put Martha Stewart to shame. She and Daniel had planned on having a lengthy engagement so they could fake her breakup with Jack and let the media circus die down a bit. But even Daniel's careful planning didn't take into account the fact that Ivy would get pregnant.

"Are you ready to head back out to the dance floor?" Daniel asked.

Ivy patted her rounded belly. Lucia had custom-tailored the gown to include room for two. It was still the wedding dress of her dreams just... bigger. "I think me and baby need a little more time to rest, if you don't mind."

Daniel settled back in his seat and moved her so she was perfectly fitted against his side. "There's no place I'd rather be, my love."

Ivy breathed in the fresh air and took in the scene before her. "It's like my own personal heaven." Ivy sighed. "Have you seen Brunelli? I want to thank him again for organizing all of this."

"Are you kidding me? He loved every second of it. Last I saw him, he was telling anyone who would listen how he orchestrated all of this. And he wasn't just talking about the wedding."

"I'm glad he's enjoying himself."

Daniel leaned over so he could whisper in her ear, sending shivers down her spine. "Don't look now but I think Brunelli found his next matchmaking challenge."

Ivy followed his gaze and laughed aloud at the sight before her. Jack, looking extremely debonair in his best man tuxedo was twirling Holly, who looked incredible in her maid of honor gown. They seemed to only have eyes for each other as they danced, laughed, and flirted the night away.

"No," Ivy said with disbelief. "You don't think...that would be so perfect." She sat up so quickly, she nearly whacked Daniel in the chin.

He gently tugged her back in his arms. "If it's meant to be, they'll find each other. Just like I found you."

"But you had help from the people who love you. Otherwise who knows how long it would have taken you to come to your senses and make me your wife? You could have lost me forever."

Daniel's arms closed tighter around her. "But I did come to my senses and now you are my family." He buried his face against her neck. "And I'm never letting go."

Ivy snuggled against him, reveling in the pure magic of her wedding day and the unconditional love she'd found. "But maybe if I tell Jack that he should—"

"Oh no, you don't," Daniel said with a laugh. "They're on their own. I don't want that big mouth of yours meddling in the course of true love."

While Ivy took offense at the big mouth comment, she did agree to keep quiet—if possible—it didn't last long.

Meet the Author

Maggie Dallen is a huge fan of happily-ever-afters. She writes contemporary and YA romance and has been known to rewrite the endings to classic love stories to ensure that they end on a happy note. In Maggie's version, Ingrid Bergman does not get on the plane. She lives in Northern California and works at a yarn store to support her knitting addiction. For more info please visit maggiedallen.com.

Follow her on Twitter @Mag_Dallen.
Or connect with her on Facebook

Keep reading for a special sneak peek of the second book in the Chance
Romance series by Maggie Dallen.

The Accidental Boyfriend

Available May 24, 2016 by Lyrical Press.

Learn more about Maggie at
http://www.kensingtonbooks.com/author.aspx/31712

Chapter 1

Crayon drawings covered every inch of Holly's classroom walls. They needed to be taken down, but instead Holly sat cross-legged atop her desk, surveying the mess her second-graders had left behind.

Summer vacation technically started twenty minutes ago but she still had hours of cleanup and paperwork ahead of her before she was done for the school year. Picking up the stack of cards her students had given her as they filed out, Holly sifted through them with teary eyes. She stopped when she came to a hot pink card with a picture of Cinderella and Prince Charming on the cover.

One of her students had drawn an arrow to Cinderella and in big block letters wrote "Miss Holly" underneath. Holly's laugh sounded loud in the empty classroom. She had come to loathe the word 'princess', thanks to the girls in her class with their rabid obsession for all things Disney, but *this*...this was adorable.

And so very fitting. Clapping a hand over her mouth, Holly smothered a near-hysterical giggle. It was true, for one night she had actually thought of herself as Cinderella.

Her breathing slowed as the memory of that night came back in vivid Technicolor. Her very own Prince Charming held her in his arms beneath the twinkling lights and twirled her in time with the music on the Italian veranda. The crowd was a blur to her because she only had eyes for one man, the man she'd had a crush on for years—Jack Everett.

"Do you need a hand in here?"

Holly came crashing back to the present as Donna, the grade school principal, poked her head into her classroom.

"What? Oh, no. I got it, thanks." She scrambled off her desk and started to take down the giant panda bear poster that hung next to the chalkboard. It was the one poster she brought with her from school to school as she traveled and she'd hung it here earlier in the year when she'd taken over as a long-term substitute when old Mrs. Ferndale had been hospitalized with pneumonia.

"I'm glad I caught you," Donna said. She walked into the room and perched on the corner of one of the student's desks. A tall, heavyset woman, Donna dwarfed the small piece of furniture and made the warm, cozy classroom feel ten times smaller. "I heard from Mrs. Ferndale this morning and she's decided that she won't be coming back in the fall. She's opted to retire as I suspected she would."

Holly froze, her fingers clenching the poster so tightly that it ripped. She turned to face the other woman. She knew where this was going. This was what she had been hoping for since she moved back to her hometown of Oakdale, Ohio.

This was what she wanted. She should be excited. Holly's stomach plummeted as a sour taste filled her mouth. Sliding into the chair behind the desk, she placed her hands on her knees to keep from fidgeting. She smiled at Donna, hoping she conveyed excited anticipation.

"Oh really?" Holly said. Her voice came out slightly breathless.

Donna paused for a moment, seemingly weighing her words. "The students and their parents absolutely love you, Holly, and I know you've expressed interest in settling down here in Oakdale."

She paused, giving Holly room to respond. Holly just nodded. She didn't trust herself to speak. It was true. She'd decided to give up travel and adventure to return to her hometown in Ohio and have the life she wanted. Have the *family* she wanted.

"If you're interested," Donna said, a slow smile spreading across her face. "We would love to make your role here permanent."

Holly gasped as though surprised—as if this wasn't a possibility they'd been talking about for the past few months. But now that it was here… she broke into a cold sweat, but forced a smile to match the principal's. Of course she was nervous. Major life changes were scary. "Oh, Donna, thank you."

Donna's smile grew as she waited for Holly to say the words that would make it official. Holly took a deep breath and opened her mouth to accept and instead she heard her voice say, "I need to think about it."

The words stunned Holly almost as much as they did Donna, who was blinking at her as though she couldn't comprehend the statement. After a moment, she resumed her composure. "Of course, it's a big decision. No one would expect you to make a hasty decision."

Holly latched onto that excuse. "Exactly. I'm not the type to act impulsively." *Liar.* "I'd really like to talk it over with my family. And Benjamin, of course."

"Of course." Donna gave her a knowing look. "How are things with Benjamin?" She and Holly had become friendly since Holly joined the school and she was aware of Holly's feeling for her longtime best friend. Donna was the only person she'd told who hadn't tried to talk her out of her quest to win back her high school sweetheart.

"Good," Holly said with a bit more enthusiasm than necessary. "Great, just great." Apparently the lies were pouring out of her mouth today.

"So he wasn't upset about the picture?"

Holly's smile froze in place. The picture. It had been more than a month since her sister's wedding, yet the local newspaper was still printing pictures of the big event. To be fair, a hometown girl marrying a billionaire in a lavish wedding in Tuscany was a tad more interesting to readers than the library's latest fundraiser. But still. Let it go already, people.

Unfortunately, one of the pictures that her mother had kindly sent to the newspaper featured Holly dancing with Jack, the world-famous tech genius. They were gazing at each other in a way that might have led some viewers to the wrong conclusion. Like that they were in love or something. Which couldn't be further from the truth. She was pretty sure Jack hated her after the way that night ended—if he hadn't already forgotten about her.

She had been making such progress with Benjamin when that stupid picture was printed. "No," she said, trying not to sound as bummed as she felt. "He wasn't upset at all."

Sadly that was the truth. She hadn't expected him to be angry—it's not like they were dating—but she had hoped he'd be a tad bit jealous. Or a whole lot jealous.

Before she'd left for the wedding, she'd made it clear that she wanted to take their friendship to the next level but Benjamin was worried that dating would ruin it. And he still wasn't convinced that settling down in Oakdale was what Holly really wanted. As if moving back home and taking a teaching job at her old school wasn't evidence enough that she was serious about changing her ways.

That picture popping up in the paper certainly hadn't helped her cause.

Donna was giving her an annoyingly sympathetic look so Holly amped up the smile. "Besides, Paula Dunhop's annual Oakdale Charity Ball is coming up this weekend so I imagine my silly picture will no longer be making the news."

Donna's eyes widened in surprise and then she cringed. "Actually... that's not the picture I was referring to."

Holly's body stiffened. "What? What other picture is there?"

Donna was already digging through her gigantic purse. She brandished an issue of *People* magazine with a flourish and handed it to Holly. "Page thirteen."

As Holly flipped to the page, her stomach plummeted. What if someone had caught their—

"That certainly looks like a kiss to me," Donna said.

Holly couldn't look up at her co-worker. She was hypnotized by the image in front of her. Jack's tuxedo jacket was draped around her shoulders and she was tucked against his side. He was leaning in and she was gazing up. They weren't actually kissing but it was clear what was about to happen seconds after the shot was captured.

Holly's mind raced and, if she was being honest with herself, so was her pulse. Jack looked good. No, he looked amazing. Just looking at the picture, she was transported back to that moment—that magical, fairy tale evening, which was rapidly becoming a nightmare that would not end.

She'd been trying to forget that night for an entire month. Thirty days of trying not to think about Jack, or that kiss...or what happened after that kiss. It was like not thinking of a pink elephant once someone has told you not to. Impossible. But maybe, just maybe, she would be able to forget the playboy hottie if everyone would stop constantly reminding her of that night!

But nooooo. First her hometown paper, and now this. She slammed the offensive magazine closed and took a deep breath. What had they been talking about? Oh yes, Benjamin.

Oh no, Benjamin.

Her chest tightened and she forced herself to take a deep breath. What were the odds that he had seen the magazine? Slim to none. If there was ever a man who did not follow pop culture gossip, it was Benjamin. Although...he did have two sisters who loved gossip more than life itself. And he lived in a town that was obsessed with all things Jack Everett and the Sinclair sisters. Oh crap, if he hadn't seen it already it was just a matter of time before he did.

Her chair made a loud creaking noise as she pushed it back and hopped out of her seat. She grabbed a box that was half packed and started heading toward the door. "Donna, I should go. I've got to see Benjamin but, uh, I'll get back to you about the teaching job, okay?"

She was out the door before Donna had a chance to respond.

* * * *

Holly found Benjamin quickly. Of course she did. That was the beauty of Benjamin—he was predictable.

She met him in his driveway seconds after he pulled in. "Hey, what are you doing here?" he asked, unloading his briefcase from the passenger side of his car. "I thought I was picking you up tonight so we could celebrate the last day of school."

She should tell him about the offer for a permanent job but she couldn't seem to get the words out of her mouth. Instead, she tucked a stray curl behind her ear and sauntered over to him with a grin. "Aren't you happy to see me?" she teased. She'd meant it to sound coy, maybe trigger a bit of flirtatious banter, but he ignored the tone and answered the question.

"Of course I'm happy to see you, I'm just surprised. I thought we'd agreed on a plan for tonight."

She resisted the urge to sigh. After all, his ability to make plans and stick to them was what she liked about him. She followed him up the walkway to his front door and into the lovely comfort of his house.

He dropped his briefcase near the front door and led the way toward the kitchen. "So did Donna have any news on Mrs. Ferndale?"

"Um…." Before she could reply, Holly noticed the packed luggage sitting in the hallway. "Going somewhere?"

Benjamin never went anywhere. Ever. He was born in Oakdale and had lived there his whole life. His idea of an exotic vacation was to drive one-hour north to a state park and go camping.

"Yeah, the company is sending me to Paris for a conference. I leave in the morning."

Her mouth fell open. "Paris? Really? That's awesome."

He shrugged. "It's just a work trip."

And then it struck her, "When were you going to tell me?"

"Tonight at dinner." He glanced over to where she stood frozen in place by the doorway. "What's wrong?"

Her hands clenched at her sides. Unbelievable. Benjamin—*her* Benjamin—was finally taking a trip, and to *Paris*, of all places, and he hadn't thought to tell her, let alone invite her along.

He was watching her, his brows drawn together in concern. "Are you okay?"

"Yes," she said, a little too quickly. She cleared her throat and tried again. "So why is your work sending you on this trip?"

Benjamin worked in IT and approximately three sentences into his story about the conference, her eyes glazed over. "Just a work trip," he'd said. Just a work trip...*to the most romantic city in the world*.

Holly had laid all the groundwork. She'd dropped hints, flirted, and instigated deep, meaningful talks about the possibility of a future together. For the love of God, she had done everything short of pounce and beg him to marry her. And he couldn't even be bothered to make one romantic gesture. Did she have to do everything?

"Holly?" He was eyeing her warily, like she might spontaneously combust.

Holly forced her hands to unclench and took a deep breath. She had to get out of there before she lost it. She had spent the past few months trying to prove to Benjamin that she had matured since they'd last dated, way back in high school, and that she was now emotionally stable and even-keeled.

Picking her purse back up from the table where she'd just set it down, she feigned a calm she did not feel. "I think we should take a rain check on dinner. You're going to need your sleep before the big trip and I've had a long day." She faked a loud yawn as she reached for the door. She would walk out of there without causing a scene if it killed her.

* * * *

Later that night Holly was camped out on the couch in her apartment. After living out of suitcases for so many years, she'd learned to get by with the necessities, which meant that all of her earthly belongings barely filled the spacious loft's closet. Her parents had given her their old couch and she'd invested in a good bed. Other than that, her place was depressingly spare.

It was more depressing than ever tonight, with Chinese food cartons scattered around the couch and an empty bottle of wine beside her. What was she doing with her life? That was the theme of this particular pity party. Had she made the wrong decision coming back here to this town? To Benjamin?

Maybe. But what was the alternative? To go back to the life she had been living, a life filled with adventure and travel and new experiences... and men just as flaky and afraid of commitment as she was. While men like that led to a fun time—okay, a *really* fun time—she wanted more from a relationship than one-night stands or casual flings. She was ready for a commitment.

She and Benjamin didn't have the kind of mad, passionate love that her sister had found with her new husband, but so what? Passion wasn't everything. Holly and Benjamin had history and, more importantly, trust. Weren't her parents always telling her that was the foundation for a solid marriage? She and Benjamin could be happy together. She just had to make him see it.

If he wouldn't woo her, she would have to do it herself. Adrenaline erased the lazy malaise she'd been wallowing in all evening. She sat up straight and threw off the quilt she'd been huddled under. She'd never been one to sit by and let an opportunity pass her by, why would she start now? Flipping open her laptop, she started to assemble a plan.

Fingers flying over the keyboard, she sorted through flights with a well-practiced eye. Her heart raced with excitement. She would be alone with Benjamin in the most romantic place in the world.

Her traitorous mind flashed on a certain villa in Tuscany. One of the most romantic places in the world, she mentally amended.

She took a deep breath and hit "buy ticket."

Paris, here I come.